TALON

SEALs of Steel, Book 4

Dale Mayer

Books in This Series:

Badger: SEALs of Steel, Book 1
Erick: SEALs of Steel, Book 2
Cade: SEALs of Steel, Book 3
Talon: SEALs of Steel, Book 4
Laszlo: SEALs of Steel, Book 5
Geir: SEALs of Steel, Book 6
Jager: SEALs of Steel, Book 7
The Last Wish: SEALs of Steel, Book 8

TALON: SEALS OF STEEL, BOOK 4
Dale Mayer
Valley Publishing Ltd.

ISBN-13: 978-1-773360-80-5
Print Edition

About This Book

When an eight-man unit hit a landmine, all were injured but one died. The remaining seven aim to see his death avenged.

Talon's best friend's murder ties in with the landmine incident. Talon walked away from Clary a year ago. She was his best friend's sister, and he vows to keep her safe.

Clary regrets losing Talon, but love—not trouble—needs to be his reason for staying…even if sending him away jeopardizes her life.

Sign up to be notified of all Dale's releases here!

http://dalemayer.com/category/blog/

Your Free Book Awaits!

KILL OR BE KILLED

Part of an elite SEAL team, Mason takes on the dangerous jobs no one else wants to do – or can do. When he's on a mission, he's focused and dedicated. When he's not, he plays as hard as he fights.

Until he meets a woman he can't have but can't forget. Software developer, Tesla lost her brother in combat and has no intention of getting close to someone else in the military. Determined to save other US soldiers from a similar fate, she's created a program that could save lives. But other countries know about the program, and they won't stop until they get it – and get her.

Time is running out… For her… For him… For them…

DOWNLOAD a ***complimentary*** copy of MASON? Just tell me where to send it!

http://dalemayer.com/sealsmason/

PROLOGUE

TWENTY MINUTES AFTER leaving the craziness at the hotel, Talon Lore knocked at the front door but didn't wait to walk into Laszlo's small Santa Fe rented house.

Laszlo was already there, working on the dead hired gun's laptop. Laszlo waved to Talon and said, "Put on your own coffee."

Talon snorted. "We walked out and left Erick to deal with the cops."

"That's all right," Geir said as he walked inside from the back door without so much as knocking. "If there was ever anybody who could handle it, it'd be Erick."

Talon studied his friend. "How are you holding up?"

Geir extended both hands, still shaking with fury. "I didn't dare go in that room."

Talon nodded. "I understand. It's all okay though. We're working our way through this. One new fact at a time."

"And faster than I would have thought," Laszlo said. "It's just these hiccups are pretty damn ugly."

"I'm also pissed you guys didn't tell me right away what you were doing," Geir said. "I had to hear after the fact."

"Hey," Talon said, "you went silent. We've been trying to reach you."

"Besides," Laszlo added, "we all heard after the fact, in a

way. Badger wouldn't ever let it go. It's been bugging him for the last two years. He caught the first lead, and we carried on down the rabbit hole from there."

Geir nodded. "Just so long as I'm in the loop from here on in."

"You're in," Talon said. "But remember, you may not want to be."

"Like you guys," Geir said, "my life hasn't moved forward. It always felt so wrong, and I couldn't find a way to get back on track."

"Well, we might have something to help you get there." Laszlo lifted his gaze from the laptop. "Because there's a lot of stuff here. It looks like we have more than enough information to confirm this John Smith asshole was a very busy boy. Not just with our cases but others. The police will still want to see this laptop. But I want to get all the information I need off it first."

"Does it say who he did business with?"

"A couple people could be in here. It's in code, and it'll take us some time. Do we have any specialists we can bring in?"

Geir snorted. "If Levi doesn't have them, you know Mason will."

Talon nodded. "And what about my friend Chad? Is there any sign this hired gun had anything to do with Chad's accident?"

Laszlo nodded. "Yes." He looked up. "I don't know how well you know the family. Do you want to say anything to them about it or let it lie in peace after all this time?"

Talon winced. "His sister and I were a thing for a long time, and Chad was my best friend. I feel like I owe her the truth for the sake of both of them."

"Clary?" Geir asked. "I remember you mentioning her a couple times. Why did you break it off?"

Talon shrugged. "Because I couldn't leave the military at the time. And she wanted me home every night," he admitted. "And I let her go because she wanted so much more than I could give her."

"How do you feel about her now?" Laszlo looked up from the laptop again, his gaze piercing, even in the darkly lit room.

"I've never forgotten her," Talon said. "But she married soon after we broke up. I figured she was more than ready for the change."

"Well, maybe it's time to renew that acquaintance."

He shook his head. "No, she's happily married. I don't want to burst that bubble."

Laszlo snorted, his fingers busy on the keyboard. "No, she's not. She got divorced last year."

Talon straightened ever-so-slightly. "Really?"

Laszlo nodded. "Really. And I think she deserves to know the truth. At least what we know of the truth. Chad was walking in a parking lot and was struck by a hit-and-run driver."

"Another vehicular accident," Geir said softly. "Son of a bitch."

Laszlo snorted. "Talon, looks like you're up next."

Talon nodded. "Maybe I am at that."

CHAPTER 1

DEPLANING IN SAN Diego, Talon grabbed his bag off the luggage cart and hefted it over his shoulder. He knew exactly where he was going. It had been almost eleven months ago since he'd been here. Almost another year of additional pain, another year of additional growth, another year of additional physical struggles. But he had survived. He had been here before, after his best friend had died a year ago. At the time Talon had considered it a senseless accident, one of those things that cut down the good people without care, without worry, striking without thinking about who the person was, individually and to others.

And now Talon had recently found out that Chad, his best friend, had been murdered. The news hadn't settled easily. Talon thought potentially this was just another bad joke in the *Life isn't fair* context. Instead it was yet one more horrible puzzle piece in a game someone else was playing to systematically take out family members and friends of the remaining members of his former SEALs unit.

Talon didn't have any close family. He knew his birth parents must be out there somewhere, but he had no idea who they even were. He had never had any inclination to seek them out. And they had never sought him out either. As far as Talon was concerned, that was fine by him.

Consequently Talon had been in and out of the foster

care system and had joined the navy as soon as he could. It had been straight upward for him after that. But, while in high school, he'd met Chad. And that had been a relationship that he had managed to keep ever since. Until Chad's murder a year ago. Talon hadn't made it for the funeral, having been in and out of the hospital from his own traumatic experience. He'd tried hard, but the doctors had refused, stating that any long-distance travel like that would set back what little progress Talon had made after yet another surgery. He was not doing well at all. The news of Chad's death had sent Talon into a tailspin. So the doctors had returned Talon to intensive care to block out the wider world until he recovered, knowing that any more bad news would potentially put him in a permanent downward spiral.

Still, he should have contacted Clary after Chad's death. When he had finally been released from the hospital weeks later, he'd made the trek alone to Chad's grave site. Against doctors' orders. But to hell with that. Chad had been the best buddy Talon had ever had. In fact, Chad had been family to Talon. Chad and Clary both. It stung like hell to have Chad ripped out of Talon's life when Talon had been at his lowest ebb yet. Even lower than when he and Clary had broken up. Or maybe it was as low as that, just doubled. Regardless the total tally of those three huge stressors in his life was more than Talon could take, one on top of the other on top of yet more. If not for the remaining members of his unit, he'd feel very alone.

Talon had stood there at the grave, hating the waste of it all. For someone like Chad—healthy and vibrant, with such a great sense of humor, always pulling jokes on everyone, a ladies' man, and yet, at the core, a good man—to have died like that, in a senseless accident, was a maddening event in and of itself. Chad was a fireman. He lived, ate, talked, slept that job. Talon laughed at the memory of Chad saying that all he had to do to get the ladies' attentions was tell them he could cook or that he wore a uniform or to just show them the firemen's calendar, sporting Chad as the Favored Fireman for February. Chad was one of the good guys—a hero.

Talon knew the two siblings had a hard time understanding their vagabond researching parents. To Talon, who had never had the stable home life that those two had, he thought their parents were great, idiosyncrasies and all. Those two didn't know how good they had it. Yeah, their mom and dad had wanted both kids to attend college, to become botanists like them, but it just wasn't meant to be.

Talon shook his head. What was it about families? They could be your greatest supporters or your worst critics. Sometimes both. *Kind of like we can do to ourselves, what with the negative and positive self-talk going on in my own mind at times.*

And there Talon was, after the land mine explosion he had miraculously lived through, thinking for the longest time that his own survival wasn't worth all this pain and effort and expense. Missing a hand, missing an arm, he was so much less than he'd been before. Plus he felt a special responsibility that his other team members didn't.

Talon had been driving the military transport truck with his unit all aboard and had driven over the buried antitank land mine.

He'd gone through the depths of depression, self-pity, and had come out on the other side, mended but still broken inside. Still dealing with nightmares. Still dealing with the trauma of so much he'd been through. Some things in life you just didn't recover from overnight. Luckily he had had his unit around him, telling him to buck up and to get well soon. That they were waiting on him, slowly gathering in Santa Fe to be closer to the prosthetics designer. They encouraged Talon, goaded Talon, whatever it took to keep that flame of survival lit within him. Even while in excruciating pain themselves.

Even while the other six members of his unit were also going through their own trials by fire, their own personal hells with hospitals, surgeries, rehab—another word for *torture*—and more hospitals, surgeries, rehab, they had still been there for Talon. They took turns visiting his bedside, depending on who was feeling the best at the time and could travel between the various hospitals where some of their unit remained hospitalized.

Talon's team members were his light at the end of a very long and very dark and very hazardous tunnel. No telling how many times each of them had died on the operating table. But Talon didn't ask. He didn't want to know. He was just happy they were still here with him. Then Talon had met Kat, and she had dangled the possibility of specially designed prosthetics to replace his arm and his lower leg. That became his goal. Get better so he could wear two of Kat's incredible designs.

Talon had to wonder how his birth parents would have handled such an event. Hell, how would Chad and Clary's parents have handled it? *Not well, I suppose.* He was again damn thankful for his unit. They were his true family.

And then his SEALs unit had realized that their military accident had been no accident. That their truck had been deliberately diverted to a new route, by a fake Corporal Shipley, based on falsified intel, where Talon's team would drive over an antitank land mine buried just for them. Seven men horribly disfigured and maimed. And one of their own dead.

Talon knew evil existed. He couldn't be in the military or experience any war and not see evil. But he also knew there was a lot of good in the world too. He wanted to believe there was good in everyone, but it was hard to see it in some people. And in the murderers, drug dealers, human traffickers … well, it was almost impossible.

To have Chad's life cut short was just denying the world the other lives that Chad would have rescued from future fires. Just like cutting down Talon's unit with that explosion would cost other people their lives down the road.

Talon was fighting to look ahead, to look forward. Yet, so far, life kept turning him around, pointing him to the past. Talon had wondered about that explosion himself over the last couple years, but he had shoved it off to the side. Yet it kept nagging him. After all, three military trucks were headed to one destination. So why did just the one truck—the one with Talon and his unit—get pulled off to another route because of last-minute intel?

Dealing with his own injuries, his own recovery, had been enough. Too much, in fact. Unlike his friend Badger, Talon hadn't used the need for revenge to get himself back on his feet. But once he understood what Badger was doing, and the amount of thought he'd put into it, his reasoning and logic behind it, Talon hadn't taken long getting on board.

That Norway trip with Cade and Laszlo had been a wake-up call in so many ways.

Cade had been blessed enough to meet somebody, a pilot who'd been in Norway dealing with her own trauma as her best friend had been in a car accident as well. But her friend was now out of a coma, and Faith and Cade were working their way through a relationship that held such promise. Talon was happy for his friend.

He'd pushed back on all steady relationships for many years. Long before the land mine incident, the love of his life had wanted more than Talon could give, so he'd walked away to let her have exactly what she said she wanted. She'd married, and he'd only recently learned she'd also divorced.

A hard hand slapped his shoulder. He turned and smiled at Laszlo who was accompanying him on this trip, telling him, "You never did give me an update on your father."

Laszlo beamed. "The old man is pretty tough. He's back home again with Jair. The two of them are living a quiet life at the moment."

"Did you tell him the hit-and-run wasn't an accident?"

"Yes, and he took it well, considering. One of Mason's friends is a bodyguard in Norway. He's moving in with my father and brother for a while, replacing the temporary help we had for them in the interim. The fact that Mason's guy happens to love cooking is a big bonus. At least I can see both men eating now."

"That will help."

Talon had been one of the trio of men who had flown to Norway to Laszlo's father's home to sort out what exactly had happened after that hit-and-run. It had seemed like a bad accident perpetrated on a dark road at dusk with an old man who had left his hearing aid at home and who couldn't have evaded the vehicle fast enough anyway. Only, in the light of day, it had been found to be a hit-and-run to hurt Laszlo. The now deceased John Smith had been hired to use an SUV and run down Laszlo's father. But not the man who had hired Smith for this job and others. Therefore, everybody who could be on this unknown killer's list, those still alive, needed security.

Which meant the family members and closest friends of the remaining seven former SEALs involved in the original land mine incident.

"What would we do without Mason and Levi?" Talon asked.

"We'd find someone. We've already got several of Bullard's men pulled into play as well."

Talon nodded. "It helps restore my faith in humanity. People aren't all assholes, like this John Smith guy was."

"At least we have his laptop and access to the hired gun's emails and contacts. It could be much worse. It's up to us to stay safe until we find another line to tug."

"I'm still not sure I should be here in San Diego," Talon said. "I know I owe it to Chad, but his case has already been closed. The police won't reopen it just to confirm our latest findings, and I don't know what benefit there is to letting Clary know what happened to him."

"Wouldn't you want to know?"

"Yes, but look who we are. She doesn't live in our world. She's a paralegal and probably sees a lot of the negative side of life. But do we have to bring it any closer to home?"

Laszlo shrugged. "When we discussed this before, you thought it was a good idea."

"At the time I wasn't standing less than ten minutes away from the woman I loved," he admitted.

Laszlo chuckled. "Yeah, I can see how cold feet would get to you. Do you realize we've been standing here for at least ten minutes, and people are walking around us because we're in the way?"

Startled, Talon twisted to look around, and, indeed, they were like an island with waves of water parting to wrap around them. He shrugged. "Let's grab a vehicle."

They headed to the airport rental office. Talon had ordered a Jeep Wrangler. It was pretty hard not to drive that vehicle, as it was, by far, his favorite. The day was warm and sunny. With Laszlo's help, Talon took off the top. He hopped in with the paperwork in hand, turned on the engine, and slowly settled in to drive. They headed toward the center of town.

"Are we stopping anywhere else?" Laszlo asked. "I mean, Mason's here. Maybe we should stop by?"

"We'll see how it goes." Talon shifted in his seat. "Damn, I do like these vehicles. I bought my first one when I was sixteen. My foster parents completely forbade me, but I bought it off the machine shop guy in high school. I worked off half of it and paid the rest with my part-time job. They had no say in the matter. But it was another huge bone of contention and another good reason to leave."

"What did you do with it when you left for the military?"

"I kept it a while, for when I was on leave, but then, after I split up with Clary, I sold it. The clean break seemed like the best idea."

"And how do you feel about that now?"

Talon decided not to answer.

After a few minutes of silence, Laszlo asked, "Did you let her know you were coming?"

Talon winced. "No. I deliberately didn't."

Laszlo checked his watch. "It's a Saturday at eleven in the morning. Any idea where she'll be?"

"She and her brother had a house they co-owned. Chad

was living in it when she moved out to get married, I presume. I thought I'd check there first."

"But it could have been sold after his death."

"It could have been. But, considering her divorce and the death of her brother, both occurring at about the same time, I suspect she would have hung on to it."

"Sentimental type?"

"Very. Her parents are in Europe most of the time. Her father is a botanist, studies plants. They own the house next door. With them gone so much of the year, it also makes sense that Clary would have retained ownership of her house. She can effectively oversee both. So it follows to check if somebody is there."

They pulled into a Starbucks, each of them grabbing coffees for the road. Talon kept driving, finally hitting the outskirts, turning into a nice suburban area, noting that, after all this time, it looked more upscale than he remembered. New eyes, new perspective.

As he drove up to the place, no vehicle was parked in either driveway. He drove past, turned around, and parked on the opposite side of the street. First they went to Chad's house and knocked. There was no answer. Then they went to the neighboring house, where Chad and Clary's parents lived, and again there was no answer.

Talon turned to look at Laszlo and shrugged. "I guess it's time to call her."

"And chances are you'll only be able to leave a message because who knows where she is."

Laszlo was right. A quick phone call later had no benefit but to leave a message.

Laszlo glanced at him. "Where do you want to go now?"

"Chad's grave," he said quietly. "I visited it a month after his death a year ago, but I'd like to go back."

They were a good twenty minutes away from the cemetery. He drove up the long winding road and parked at the lower end of the parking lot. "If my memory serves me correctly, his grave is at the bottom end."

They got out and walked toward that area. It was a beautiful day and, outside of the reason for being here, it was a great place to be right now. Talon tilted his head toward the sun, letting the rays shine on his face. "Definitely nicer weather here," he said.

Laszlo chuckled. "Sure beats Norway."

It took a little bit of walking to find the place. But soon enough Talon stopped beside the family plot. Chad was buried beside his grandparents. Clary was supposed to be laid to rest beside him and their parents on either side.

Talon stood here for a long moment, his hands in his pockets. Laszlo stepped back and gave him some space. Talon appreciated that. Of all the men in his unit, Laszlo was the most sensitive to moods. It was tough. There was always something in these last couple years that would send Talon's emotions off the wall. He tried hard, but it wasn't the easiest.

After a few moments he could feel a great big breath wallop from his heart and chest. As he slowly exhaled, he felt some of the weight coming off his shoulders. "I'm so sorry, Chad. I thought, at the time, it was just life being a bitch. But now I realize it's humanity that's a bitch. Don't you worry. We caught the bastard. Not in time for you, but, maybe by doing what we've done, we can stop more deaths."

Aware of a presence beside him, Talon turned, expecting to see Laszlo. Instead a woman stared at him. Shock, anger, and pain were on her face.

"Talon?"

He hunched his shoulders, not only against the shock and accusation in her voice but also to ward off the pain of seeing her again. She had one of those baby-doll faces with curly blond ringlets and huge blue eyes. He'd been dumbstruck from the first time he had met her. He thought he'd done her a favor by walking away, and obviously she'd made good use of the time because she had quickly married. He was sorry it hadn't worked out for her.

He nodded his head and said, "Hi, Clary."

She motioned to her brother's grave. "Why now?" Her voice was angry. "Why not a year ago when he actually died? A little too late, isn't it?"

He took the blows, but they hit him at a visceral level. He could give her no excuses, as he had no intention of trying to explain. He turned to his side and motioned toward Laszlo. "I'm here with a friend of mine. Laszlo Jensen. This is Clary Witcher."

She glanced over at Laszlo and gave a small head tilt of acknowledgment then zeroed back in on Talon. "That's no excuse. You could've come any time in the last year."

There was so much hurt in her voice, and he knew it had been a tough year for her. And he should have been here for her. Just like he would have loved it had she'd been there for him. But nobody outside his unit had been there for him because he hadn't told anybody. Only somehow Chad had found out, and Talon wasn't even sure how that had happened. Chad had lit into Talon at the hospital something fierce. But apparently Chad hadn't told Clary about Talon's condition. And, for that, Talon was glad that he had made Chad promise not to.

She was always the kind of person who brought home an abandoned kitty or a lost puppy. And he had no intention of being added to her collection. He didn't say anything, just looked at her, drinking in her features so familiar and yet with just enough differences to make his heart ache. She'd had a tough couple of years, and she obviously wasn't sleeping well. There were lines on her face, her color now filled with bright red flags of anger, but the rest of her skin was so white.

"I was just at your house, Chad's house," Talon said quietly. "Are you living there now?"

She shoved her fists into her pockets and rocked back on her heels. "What do you care?" She tossed her hair back, a motion she'd always used when she was pissed off.

He had been able to get her goat all the time. It had been part of the fun, watching her explode. But they'd been so much younger back then, foolish. He dropped his gaze to the grave. "I care."

"It doesn't seem like it." She glanced again at Laszlo, held it for a moment.

Laszlo stepped forward and outstretched his hand. "It's nice to meet you."

She shook his hand stiffly. Faced Talon. "What were you saying to Chad when I arrived?"

He winced.

"TALON?" SHE SAID in a harder tone. She sensed something wrong, and her gut clenched with pain. "I heard you, but I didn't really understand you."

He turned to face her fully, and she saw the torment on his face. He really did care. She knew he did too. Talon and her brother had been friends since forever. Obviously Chad's death would be a loss for him. She had no right to throw that in his face, but it was hard because she was hurting too.

"Why don't we go for coffee somewhere and talk?"

She snorted. "You didn't come all this way to see me, so why don't you just tell me what you need to tell me, and we can part ways again."

"Wow, you got nicer as you got older."

She flushed, taking a direct hit. The trouble was, he was right. She hadn't gotten nicer; she'd gotten more independent, harder, more protective, and more hurt.

It was Laszlo who said, "Maybe not a coffee shop. I know it's an imposition, but possibly could we speak with you in your own home?"

She stared at him in surprise. "Why?"

"Because what we have to say should be said in private."

Should she trust Laszlo? It was hard when he was with Talon. Yet he had never lied to her, but something about the previous years seemed like a lie no matter what. He should have returned. She'd waited until the truth hit her—Talon was never returning.

She thought about it for a long moment and then nodded. "I'll meet you back at the house in ten minutes."

"Ten minutes?" Laszlo asked.

She flashed a small smirk. "Okay, that's just a figure of speech. It takes about twenty minutes, maybe longer. It depends on the traffic." She saw the coffee cups in their hands. "I guess I can put on coffee when I get there."

"Don't do us any favors if your heart is not in it," Talon said calmly.

But there was such a neutrality to his tone and in his expression, as if he expected something from her, and she hadn't given it. Trouble was, she didn't know if it was a hug or a slap that he thought he deserved. She knew which one *she* thought he deserved.

She turned and walked back to the parking lot. Inside her nerves and stomach twisted constantly. She didn't know what she was supposed to do, but her hands shook so hard, as if she would never calm them down. Her heart hurt; tears threatened, but her world … It had shattered. Just when she thought nothing else could make her life any more bereft, Talon had to show up, standing in front of her, uncaring, unaffected, and completely disinterested.

Since when had life become such a bitch?

CHAPTER 2

SHE UNLOCKED HER front door and walked inside. She didn't know why she was using the front door. Normally she would come in through the garage. She put it down to being so flustered at her current state of affairs. The men hadn't pulled in behind her, but she knew they wouldn't get lost. Talon had come to this area more times than he'd actually gone home.

This house hadn't been their parents' home but their uncle's. And, when he died, he had passed it on to the two kids. The idea being that, when her parents passed, she'd end up with one, and her brother would end up with the other. And now? … Well, now there was just her.

She didn't dare let her mind go down that route. The last year had been brutal. It was one thing to lose a sibling; it was another thing to lose a twin. And she knew a lot of people wouldn't understand, but another twin would. There was a special bond. They'd always understood each other.

And she and Chad had been very close. He'd tried to talk her out of getting married but then had stood up for her when she'd walked down the aisle. He'd held her in his arms during her breakup, and then he had died and left her alone.

Without her husband, thank God; without her parents, who were traveling the world and always would be traveling the world; and without Talon. The one mainstay in her life who'd walked away from her because she'd been too needy.

What a lesson that had been. The reason her husband had divorced her, supposedly, had been because she'd been too detached, too unemotional, not invested in their marriage. The trouble was, he was right. She'd invested everything in Talon, and, when he'd broken up with her, he had left her in tiny pieces.

It wasn't fair. She'd loved that man to distraction. And when he had walked away, it had been her brother who had helped her pull herself together. And she had built herself up bigger and stronger and better and so much tougher. She hid behind a wall so nobody would hurt her again, and, by doing so, she'd cheated her husband from feeling the full effects of her love. And she had loved him. But she hadn't been *in love* with him.

She'd been desperate to not be an old maid on the shelf, lonely for someone to do things with. She'd fallen on a path that, like everybody else's relationship, seemed to lead to marriage, to starting a family. But it didn't spark a fire in her. He was just comfortable. She thought comfortable would be enough. And maybe, for her, it would have been for years to come. But again she didn't get that chance. Her husband had walked out, saying she was only half of a woman. That she lacked passion; she lacked soul.

His words had hurt. Even now as they'd taken root, they made her doubt herself all over again. Two major relationships, and, in both cases, each man had broken up with her. So definitely there was something wrong. The stupid thing was, each of them had complained about the opposite thing.

The doorbell rang just as she hit the coffee machine's button to start brewing. She walked to the front door and opened it. The two men stood there. She led them inside, into the living room. As soon as they were seated, she said, "I'll go get you a coffee."

She turned, leaving them as guests in the house, and went to the kitchen, where she poured two cups. She carried them to the front of the house, saying, "I hope black is fine. I don't have any cream, although I might be able to find the sweetener for you."

Talon didn't say a word; he accepted the black coffee. But she knew he always used to love his coffee dark and strong.

Laszlo smiled and said gently, "Black is fine. Thanks."

She returned to the kitchen, grabbed herself a cup, then sat on a third chair in the living room. "Now tell me what this is all about."

Silence fell hard and heavy.

Her gaze went from one to the other, sharp, intense, confused. "Talon, what the hell's going on?" She watched a flicker of emotion cross his face. But she wasn't sure what that emotion was.

He lifted his gaze to her. "Put the coffee down."

She put it down, as if his command must be met. "Is it my parents? Why haven't the police come and told me?" she asked anxiously.

He shook his head. "It's not your parents. As far as I know, they're perfectly fine."

She took a deep breath and sat back, but her coffee was still on the coffee table. "Okay, so it's major but not that major. Stop beating about the bush. This isn't like you."

She felt his gaze lock on hers and sear right into her soul. He'd always had that ability. She could never lie to him. She tried hard to bring her defenses into place, so he wouldn't see her emotions, like he always had, and knew she had failed when she saw a gentle look come into his gaze. She shook her head. "Oh no, none of that."

Surprise had him raising his eyebrows. "None of what?"

"None of that trying to be friends. I know who you really are inside that bullshit," she snapped. "Tell me what this is about." She couldn't stand the worry eating away at her. It was bad, she knew. But as long as they didn't tell her what it was, she was making it so much worse in her mind.

The two men exchanged a hard glance. She watched as Laszlo raised an eyebrow in question.

She jumped in. "Sure, you tell me then." Laszlo gave her a bland look, and she sighed. "You're as bad as he is." She turned back to Talon. "Well?"

He took a deep breath. "Chad was murdered. It wasn't an accident. He was run down on purpose."

She felt the tsunami hit her. Her body freezing, her heart stopping.

And then he said, "And it's my fault."

A cry escaped as she stared at him, wordless. Every ounce of control she'd had in finding her way back from her brother's death shattered into a million pieces. She shook her head. "Dear God, please, no." She glanced over at Laszlo. "Please, tell me that's not true."

Laszlo took a deep breath. "I'm sorry. It's true."

THERE WAS NO easy way to tell her. He had to just come out and say it. But, as he stared at her, the look in her eyes, her knees pulled up to her chest as she rocked back and forth, the tiny whimper in the back of her throat, he couldn't stay separated from her. He hopped up from his chair, reached out, and scooped her into his arms. He sat back down in her seat and tucked her in close.

Laszlo, once again being who he was, went outside to the front step. Talon could see him through the living room window. Talon just held Clary. "I'm so sorry," he whispered. "I'm so sorry."

She was like this block of ice, locked down, unable to move. But, at his words, she burst into tears. Her agony was mixed with anger. She reared back and smacked him hard across the face, then started pounding him on the chest.

And he let her. He would like to have done the same. Beat himself to a pulp for having caused her this pain, for having taken away such a generous soul as Chad.

When tears overcame her, she curled up in his arms and bawled. He gently stroked her back and just held her close. God, it had been such a long time. His reason for coming here was shitty, his reason for staying away probably even worse. But, for this moment in time, he was just grateful to have her here in his arms.

Finally she ran down, but she didn't move, as if exhausted and without any further energy. She'd always been like that. Everything she did was 100 percent. Her temper, her laughter, her passion.

There was no artifice about her. She'd been so damn real. But everything he'd seen of her so far in this last hour made him realize how difficult the last years had been. There was a hardness to her that he didn't like. He had no reason to judge her, no right to criticize her because he was no longer the same idealistic young man who would go off and save the world either.

Finally she lifted her head, looked up at him, and croaked out, "Are you sure?"

He nodded. He reached for her cup of coffee. He picked it up and held it to her lips. "Take a drink. That'll make your throat feel better."

She drank eagerly, like a child, and managed a good half cup. He put it down and tucked her against him. It was a sign of how exhausted and shocked she was that she let him. He fully expected, when she got her balance back, she would turn around and hit him again.

At that point, Laszlo walked inside and sat down. He placed his empty cup on the coffee table and waited.

She sniffled and wiped her nose with her sleeve.

Talon chuckled. "You're still doing it that way."

She shot him a look and muttered, "There isn't a tissue available."

Laszlo got up. Talon watched as his friend crossed to the side table and brought her a box of Kleenex.

"Thank you," she said, taking one to blow her nose. As she did so, she realized where she was sitting. She crawled off his lap, picked up her coffee cup, and disappeared into the kitchen.

Laszlo said, "That went well."

"Of course it didn't. But then there was no easy way to tell her, was there?" Talon said in a low tone.

Just then she returned, her coffee cup filled. She sat down in Talon's original seat. "When did you find out?"

"Yesterday," Talon said quietly. "We only found out yesterday."

"You're sure?"

This time Laszlo answered. "Yes, we're sure. Chad was run over by the same guy who ran down my father in Norway during his evening walk."

She gasped. "This man killed both of them? In two

countries?"

For Talon it was yet another reminder of how much her world didn't touch the much darker, deeper world he lived in.

Laszlo said, "My father is still alive. At seventy-four, he's doing remarkably well, considering the damage done to his body. But it was because of him that we went to see if it really was an accident or if it was attempted murder. We tracked that same asshole back to Santa Fe and found out every one of us in our old military unit has lost—or, in my case, almost lost—a family member. Talon had no blood family to lose, but he'd lost Chad, his best friend."

"And the next best thing to family that he had," she said, nodding in understanding. "That's a lot of hate. What did you guys do to this guy?" she asked, her gaze going from one to the other.

Laszlo said, "We have no idea. Quite possibly your brother was the first. We don't know."

Talon spoke up. "No, Badger's parents died six months after the accident."

"What accident?" she asked.

Talon froze. He hadn't meant for her to know about it.

She stared at him, and her voice deepened. "*What* accident, Talon?"

Again Laszlo stepped in. "The same accident that injured all seven of our unit, including Talon, and killed one of our members." His voice slowed as he said, "That was two years ago."

She stared from one to the other. "How bad was the accident?"

Laszlo glanced over at Talon. "There's no point in hiding it."

Talon knew this was yet another turning point. But there was no help for it. He wasn't the man he had been. Slowly he took the glove off his prosthetic left hand for her to see. "Bad enough," he said quietly. "I'm also missing my lower left leg and foot."

She stared at him in shock and then burst into tears yet again.

CHAPTER 3

WHEN SHE COULD, she asked in a low tone, "Why didn't you tell us?"

He gave her a flat stare and said, "Because I didn't want your pity. Because I had a difficult journey of my own, and I didn't want anybody mocking me or feeling like I was less than I should be."

She shook her head in disbelief. "You know that's not something we'd ever do."

"Maybe not you, maybe not Chad, but there are certainly people who take great delight in demeaning others who have a difficult path to walk," he said. "Besides, Chad knew."

That blow almost felled her. "What?"

He nodded. "I don't know how he found out. I had been planning on going hiking with him when I came back from my last tour. I was due back in ten days. When I didn't arrive, he checked and kept checking to see where I was. Finally he hounded somebody into telling him that I'd been in a bad accident. When he eventually tracked me down, he forced his way in, until he could be at my bedside in the hospital, finding out for sure if I was alive or not. I was only a few shades away from dead actually," he said in dry humor. "And I forbade him to tell you."

She stared at him again in shock. "Why?" she asked bewildered. "Why couldn't he tell me?"

"For the same reason as before. I didn't want him telling anyone."

She glared at him. "Right now I just want to walk over there and smack you hard."

He raised an eyebrow. "And you probably would have if I hadn't shown you my hand. But already you've seen me as handicapped. Somebody you have to protect and to treat better."

"You will never be handicapped," she snapped. "You're too arrogant, too strong, too powerful, too determined."

Laszlo chuckled. "I see you know him well."

She shot him a glance. "I know him *too* well. He's insufferable most of the time."

"And the rest of the time?" Laszlo asked with a grin. "Apparently he's not that bad."

She shook her head, turned toward Talon. "You still should have let him tell me."

"Why? So you wouldn't have hated me all these years?"

She glared at him. "The only time I really hated you was when you didn't show up for Chad's funeral. At the time I thought you hadn't had anything to do with him in the previous years either, since we broke up. I'd spoken to him about you, but he never said a word." Her tone carried her frustration. "What was I supposed to think when you didn't show up? I couldn't even tell you myself because I didn't have your contact information."

He didn't say a word.

She raised both hands in frustration. "And you never explained yourself. It's as if you think I don't have a right to know."

"It's not that you don't have the right to know," Laszlo interjected, "but the news will upset you yet again."

"What are you talking about?"

Laszlo smiled. "He won't tell you, but I will," he said, ignoring the expression on Talon's face. "At the time of Chad's death, Talon had just come from a very difficult surgery where he died on the table. He was in critical care and found out somehow what had happened to Chad. Talon was in a spiral downward that almost took his life again as he tried to fight off the drugs and fight off the surgery so he could come to Chad's side.

"At that point, the doctors knocked him out and kept him sedated for several days, as he was a danger to himself. Then, when he did wake up, he wasn't allowed to have any contact with the outside world for at least another ten days, until he stabilized. When he was released from the hospital a month later, he managed to evade all of us and came here on his own and went to Chad's grave site. After he had a chance to visit, he went back into the hospital because he'd already reinjured himself again."

She sank back, tears slowly sliding down her cheeks. Hearing Laszlo's recital and seeing Talon's downcast face and the white-knuckled grip he had on the arm of the chair, she realized that Laszlo was telling the truth. She'd been so wrong. She'd jumped to the wrong conclusion, thinking that, when Talon had walked away, he'd walked away from her and from Chad.

But instead he'd stayed in close contact with Chad, and her brother had found out about Talon's life-threatening injuries and fought to be at his side. Whereas she hadn't even bothered. She'd been so hung up on her marriage and divorce that it had never occurred to her that something really bad could have happened to Talon. She shook her head, hating herself at that moment. And him because he could have made it easier on both of them. "You should have told me," she said. "I've never judged you."

Instantly she felt bad because, of course, it was a lie. That was exactly what she'd done. She'd wanted him to leave the military and to be with her all the time. She'd been young, foolish, idealistic. She hadn't realized one had to love and one had to let go. He had a mission, and he was one of the few men capable of doing the kind of work he did. And it was a crime to everyone else if he couldn't do it because he was so damn good at it. But she hadn't given him that chance.

She'd given him an ultimatum instead, and he'd released her to find someone else. At the time all she'd done was get angry and hurl mental insults at him. Because she'd been hurting so bad. Chad had tried to talk to her about it, explain what she'd done and why it had been so wrong. But she didn't want to listen. All she wanted was Talon back. What she should have done was said he was welcome to do what he felt he needed to do, and she was there for him.

Now as an adult, not an immature twenty-one-year-old girl, she got it. "I would have understood," she said quietly. "I'm not that stupid girl anymore. I do understand that life has ups and downs and that it's not all sunshine and roses."

He stared at her but wouldn't say anything in his defense.

She'd done that to him too. She used to rail at him when he'd done things wrong, and he'd never defend himself. He would just stand there and stare at her, wait for her to finish. She'd always felt better afterward, and then she would immediately feel worse because, of course, he never would stand up for himself. He would never give an explanation.

"Why couldn't you have told me?" she asked, bewildered.

"Because," Laszlo said, "he didn't want you to see him as anything other than what he was before—strong, capable, determined, physically fit, whole."

She sagged in her chair, realizing just how hard it must have been for these men to have dealt with the accident. And, if Talon had lost an arm and a foot, she glanced over at Laszlo and asked, "And the others? Were they as badly hurt? Or was just Talon so badly injured?"

"All of us were badly hurt," Laszlo said quietly. "Some of us lost organs. Some of us lost limbs and organs. All of us lost muscle, tissue, bones, and all of us gained metal plates, metal screws, something added somewhere. All of us went through tremendous heartache, frustration, depression. Most of us hit the suicidal wall at one point. Only revenge kept our team leader, Badger, coming back from the brink."

Talon picked up the story. "And now that most of us have healed enough to live a more or less normal life, and we have now realized that our incident was quite likely not an accident, we all have a purpose again. But with that purpose comes an understanding that all of us were directly affected and, in another way now, have been further injured with the loss of friends and loved ones. And we're undertaking the difficult job of letting people know."

"Maybe you would rather have been left in the dark," Laszlo broke in. "I wasn't sure what you'd rather know. I pushed Talon to come and to tell you because we ourselves would prefer to know."

"Of course I want to know," she said warmly. "And, yes, thank you for coming and telling me. It doesn't make it any easier. In fact, it probably makes it worse, but at least I know Chad wasn't being stupid in the parking lot or unaware. He really had no chance."

"No, he didn't," Talon said. "He was targeted."

"And I have to admit," she said, feeling a huge weight come off her shoulders, "maybe it releases some of my guilt."

"Why guilt?" Laszlo asked.

"Because I was having trouble with somebody at the time, and I told Chad about it. He said he'd check into it. And he was dead three months later. At the time I was terrified it was related to him checking into my problem. And, since my problem stopped when he died, I figured that was just more proof that I had a hand in his death."

Talon leaned forward, his arms resting on his knees. "What are you talking about?"

She gave him a quick glance. "I thought I had a stalker. I kept looking around, and somebody always seemed to be there. A Lexus that kept following me. I didn't know what he wanted. I finally told Chad about him, and he said he'd see if he could find out who it was."

"A black Lexus was following you?" Talon asked.

She frowned. "I didn't tell you the Lexus was black."

"No, but we suspect the driver of a black Lexus was connected to your brother's death."

"At least it's the same type of vehicle, but that doesn't mean the same driver. We don't know anything at this point," Laszlo corrected. "Our killer *was* driving a Lexus in Santa Fe. We can't be sure it's the same one. We can't even be sure it's the same model. But he had a penchant for Lexus vehicles. Although that doesn't mean he used them to commit crimes."

She sat back. "Do you have a picture of the killer?"

Talon reached in his pocket, then stopped and glanced at Laszlo. "I left mine in my pack. Do you have a copy?"

Laszlo pulled several photos from his pocket. He handed the printed images to Clary.

"This is him," Clary said.

"This is a man we only know as John Smith."

"Right, great name." She tapped the paper with her finger. "This is one of the guys. But it's not the second one." She shuffled through the photos. "Don't you have a picture of the other one?"

Both men stared at her. In a low voice Talon asked, "Who's the other one?"

She frowned. "He's the man who started stalking me. And then this guy stepped in. I crossed paths with them at a coffee shop. They were having a conversation. When they realized I'd seen them, I didn't see the other guy anymore, and this one took over. Honestly it was the most bizarre thing." She watched as Talon and Laszlo exchanged a hard glance.

Talon turned to her. "Can you describe the other one?"

She frowned. "Why?"

"Because we think he might be the one who hired the man who killed your brother."

TALON WAITED WITH bated breath while he watched her contemplate this news.

She got up for a moment, then turned back to him and said, "Excuse me." She went into the kitchen.

They could hear her rummaging around in one of the drawers. "What is she looking for?" Laszlo asked.

"No idea," Talon answered. "But if she can identify the other man …"

"Doesn't mean he's the boss. It could be another hired gun or could be somebody who was an intermediary," Laszlo said.

"It's a line to tug. And we need any and all lines there are."

Laszlo nodded. "That's true."

"Again we don't know anything for sure at this point."

Laszlo nodded.

"That's something we can ask Mason to look into," Talon said. "We're talking a long time ago. That's the problem."

"Not all that long ago," Clary announced as she walked into the living room. She held several sketchbooks in her hands. "I thought I saw him here again about a month ago. Actually he looked straight past me, so I don't know. Maybe I imagined it."

At that news Talon bolted upright. "You saw him one month ago?"

"Maybe. I don't really know."

Talon looked at Laszlo. "Maybe the boss lives here. Maybe the Lexus is his."

"In which case, we have to talk to all the Lexus owners in town."

"Good luck with that. This is San Diego. There's got to be thousands of them here."

"I don't suppose you happen to know what model?"

She shrugged. "Black. That's all I can tell you."

The two men nodded. Laszlo brought out a notebook and jotted down some of the things she'd said.

She flipped open the top of one of her sketchbooks and held out the first picture. "This is the guy I think is in your photograph."

It was a quick rough sketch, and yet it captured the

bearded man in their photographs perfectly. As Talon looked at the drawing, he remembered just how gifted an artist she had been. But she'd never done portraits before. "Since when did you start doing faces? You always hated them."

"I hated a lot of things back then. And what I was doing wasn't working, so I decided to switch and find something that would work."

He studied her face, sensing so much more behind her words, but she wasn't giving anything away. He flipped through the pages, but they were blank. He grinned. "You still hate reusing a book, once you've drawn on the first page, don't you?"

She shrugged, self-conscious. "I've gotten better at it. I can't just keep using the top page and not the others," she admitted. "But I do tend to keep a lot of blank pages in between. The rest of that book is empty."

He handed the sketchbook to Laszlo.

Laszlo whistled. "This is really good," he said admiringly.

She chuckled. "Thanks."

"No, I mean it. This is good. Do you do this professionally?"

She shrugged. "I have an art gallery that's interested in my work. The owner has been trying to get me back to my art. He says it doesn't matter when I do the show, just to pick up a pencil again." She gave him a lopsided smile. "I told him that I wasn't sure I was staying in town, and he didn't seem to care. Said paintings were shipped all over the world."

"Chad's death?" Talon hazarded a guess.

She nodded. "I was doing a lot of artwork as a way to get through my terrible marriage. Then I got separated and lost

Chad. That kind of made me hit the brakes. It's been hard to get my mojo back."

"We both understand that," Talon said. "But you're very talented. Don't quit."

Self-consciously she opened the next sketchbook. "I saw them at the coffee shop. This is what I did afterward. I don't think you will be able to identify him from it." She handed the second sketchbook to Talon.

And again on the top page was a restaurant scene with the men farther in the distance, one very identifiable, and thankfully very dead, and the second one sitting across from him, both huddling over coffee, heads closer together as if talking privately. He studied the second man's face, then shook his head. "I don't recognize him." He handed the book to Laszlo, then froze and motioned for Laszlo to hand it over again. "I don't recognize him, but …" He lifted his gaze. "There's something almost familiar about him."

"And that's even worse," Laszlo said. "Because it'll just sit there and bug you until you figure it out." When Talon handed the image back, Laszlo took a turn, twisting the image side to side; then he glanced at Clary and asked, "Do you have any others like this?"

She shook her head. "No. I had a lot that I drew leading up to this," she admitted. "But, once I got those down, I just tossed the rest. Honestly I had forgotten about them. When Chad started to look into the issue, it just went away."

"I suspect what they did was change targets," Laszlo said.

"But why us?" Clary asked.

"No way to know for sure," Laszlo said. "You might have seen them without knowing it. They may have panicked. Before that, there was nothing to link you to them."

"My brother is a link to Talon," she protested. "Surely

that's something."

Talon nodded. "And, as long as you haven't seen anybody since, then you're probably in the free and clear."

"Except I just saw him a month ago."

"But he didn't see you, right?"

She frowned. "I don't think so. And, even if he did, I don't think he'd have recognized me. I'm not sure anybody would have recognized me actually. I'd been at a costume party and was wearing a cosplay outfit from The Legend of Zelda."

He stared at her in surprise. "Really?"

She nodded. "I went as an anime character first to the parties. Then I decided to go as Link."

Laszlo chuckled. "Depending on how well you were dressed up, maybe he didn't recognize you."

She walked over to the credenza on the far wall, where she picked up an envelope. It was a large brown business envelope. She pulled out several prints. "This is a picture of me from that night."

The two men laughed.

"That's great," Talon said. True enough she looked identical to the main character. "And you're right. He probably didn't recognize you. And that's a good thing."

"Why?"

"Because, if he didn't recognize you, he won't worry that you recognized him."

"What difference does it make?"

"Because, if he is still around, he hasn't finished his business. If he's still around, chances are he's still keeping an eye on you. Have you had that weird sensation of being stalked anymore?"

She sat down with a thump. "No, not really," she said

slowly. And then she stopped.

Talon leaned forward. "But?"

"I found the house doors unlocked a week ago, and then, a few days ago, the living room window was wide open." She shrugged. "I've never opened these living room windows, and I'm very cautious about the doors being locked because it's just me here now. I'm always looking after my parents' house and this one." Then she shrugged and said, "I'm sure it's nothing."

"Oh, it's more than nothing," Talon said, his voice hard. "As a matter of fact, I'm pretty damn sure it's a very big something."

CHAPTER 4

SHE STARED IN disbelief at Talon. "Oh no. I'm not doing that again."

"Doesn't matter if you want to or not if somebody else is making that decision for you."

"What could he possibly want from me? His partner already went after my brother."

"We were wondering that ourselves," Laszlo interjected. "Someone's already taken somebody from every one of us, except for Geir. Three *accidents* have been linked directly to John Smith, but since he's dead now, we're trying to figure out if his partner is coming back for a second round."

She stared at him. "This is just too unbelievable. Do you really think he'll come after me?"

"He started with you and was sidetracked by your brother."

"This is just too much," she cried, throwing her hands in the air. "This doesn't happen in real life."

"It is happening." Talon stood and walked to her. "And the sooner you realize it, the better. Obviously we don't know if this other guy's got plans for you, but it's something we have to take into consideration."

She shoved her jaw at him and glared mutinously. "If he was going to do something, he would have done it already."

"Not necessarily. He could have been on a recon trip.

Seeing if your house was secure. Checking if he can get in through a door or a window," Laszlo said. "Studying your routine. Seeing how you get to work and when you're off work and coming home."

She shook her head. "That was all before. That's why I asked Chad about it."

"What was all before?"

"I was seeing the same person around the gym. At the grocery store. Following me. But, since Chad's death, there's been nothing. It's like I've been in a fog since."

"This will be a hard question for you to answer," Talon said as he stepped directly in front of her. "Considering what you've been through this last year—how emotionally wrecked you've been, dealing with Chad's death, the funeral arrangements, recovering, your parents in and out of the country, your separation and divorce—would you have noticed if you were being stalked?"

She stared at him, not liking what he suggested. "So you're thinking that, because I'm such an emotional wreck, I would have missed it?" She gave it some serious thought, and then she shook her head. "I don't think so. I was really concerned at the time that Chad might have died because of me and my stalker. So I was looking forward to catching the stalker behind me wherever. To relieve my guilt. But the stalking didn't restart again."

"So he's changed his MO."

She turned to look at Laszlo. "*MO*?"

"It just means the way he does things. We can't say if you're in danger or not, but the fact that somebody left the door unlocked and somebody left a window open makes it very suspicious."

She crossed her arms over her chest. "You guys are just

full of good news, aren't you?"

"What we don't do is stick our heads in the sand. Not now that we know six of us have all had people important to us attacked because of this asshole."

"And you had no clue?"

"Not until we went to Norway, and then we began to put it all together. You have to understand. This dealt with different family members, different countries, different time periods over the last two years." Talon raised his shoulders and held out his hands, palms up. "And most of us were in and out of the hospital, trying to recover from our own massive injuries. Who would suspect anyone of taking out our family members on purpose?"

"You must have some clue who's doing this? I know some of your work was dangerous. Isn't there somebody specifically who you pissed off?"

Laszlo shook his head. "We pissed off lots of people. But it wasn't just us. Keep in mind, we were in the navy, on missions we were ordered to go on. Some of them were highly secretive. All of them were very dangerous. We helped governments go up and down. We rescued kidnapped victims. We helped move people to safety after insurgents fired on villages. We were involved in a lot of things. But for one person to target us specifically …"

"But why does it have to be one person?" she asked. "Maybe it's a group. Maybe they sent over a special unit to take you guys out." She thought it was a reasonable assumption and could see the men were at least giving it some thought. But she also recognized the moment it was dismissed as not being of value. She sighed. "Okay, so what if it is one person. That's a lot of hate. Like I said before, to come after each and every one of you and then to go after family members, … this is somebody you know."

"It'll be somebody we know," Laszlo said. "But what we don't know is why he's doing it."

"That's just not … It's wrong." She couldn't come up with any better word. But to think somebody was targeting and had killed multiple people was just unbelievable.

"He's also playing with us," Talon said suddenly. "He rented a vehicle using as his middle name the nickname of one of us, the one man in our unit who died."

She stared at him in confusion. "He used that name thinking maybe you guys would find out?"

"That's what I figure," Talon said. "He used it as a joke. Except we would understand it really was him. It's partly how we put this all together."

"And maybe he started doing that because you were so slow to pull it together," she snapped. "Now it's a case of him thinking, *Finally you're there*, and you understand he's there too."

"Something like that, yes," Laszlo said. "But, in our defense, you have to remember how we've been in and out of hospitals. Some of us were unconscious for periods of time. Many of us were not even physically capable of moving and had to learn from scratch how to do the simplest things. Our minds, in some cases, were very sharp, others not so sharp. But our physical bodies had taken a beating."

"Do you think he understood how badly injured you all were?"

Silence. Laszlo and Talon frowned at each other.

"I don't know," Laszlo said. "I'm not sure how much information the hospital would have given out on our conditions. And, if people were constantly calling to find out, would that make them suspicious?"

"Not once the media got wind of it," Talon said. "Because they called all the time, interested in the war stories of returning soldiers, especially the wounded warriors who had paid the biggest price for our country."

"Who told you about Chad's death?" she asked suddenly.

He looked at her and frowned. "I can't remember. Why?"

"Because he wanted to hurt you – toy with you," she said. "You were already recovering, and he killed somebody, but where's the fun in it if you don't know?"

She hated the brilliant anger that lit up his gaze. She could see his jaw locked down tight as he contemplated her words. It was almost like a blow to his heart, something she could see.

Laszlo leaned toward Talon. "Does that work?"

"It's possible," Talon admitted. "But I honestly don't remember now. That was before the drugs wore off and my collapse. I remember shouting about Chad being dead. Then the nurse was there, me fighting her off. I was injected with something to knock me out. But, when I woke up, I remembered he was dead, but I didn't know anything about the details." He frowned. "I don't think I had a phone." He stared at Laszlo. "Why is it I never thought of that before?"

"Talon, we've had a lot of shocks the last few years. It'll take a long time for all the bits and pieces to come back. Don't knock yourself if you didn't know ahead of time."

"But, if you can remember now, it might at least give you a starting point," Clary said. "And I highly doubt you've changed that much. The thing you always needed to do was have something to work on, a mission. I can see how revenge might have kept you all going, but this needs a whole lot more than vengeful thinking. This needs a plan."

HE WAS CAUGHT in the fog of memories, trying to figure out how he had first learned about Chad's death. He wanted to say it was a phone call. But was it? And who would have called to let him know? He'd been swimming in and out of the pain, just surfacing enough to be cognizant of the nurses. His cell phone wasn't even with him back then. He'd lost it in the land mine accident and hadn't gotten a new one until months after his recovery. He'd been completely cut off from the world for a long time. He thought one of his friends had brought a cell phone in for him. But it wasn't then—it was much later.

"I feel like somebody told me. Like I can hear the voice in my ear."

"What does the voice sound like?"

He turned to Clary. There was something almost shocking about what was going through his mind. He turned to Laszlo. "It's not possible, is it?"

He could see Laszlo's mind working the angles, figuring it out himself. "I won't say it's not possible," Laszlo said. "It would be diabolical. And that certainly fits."

"I don't understand," Clary said. "Don't race ahead on me here. I need to understand what you're talking about."

"I'm wondering if the asshole who had your brother killed walked into the hospital, stepped into my room, and told me in person," Talon admitted. "I didn't have a phone. My phone was destroyed in the land mine explosion, along with everybody else's. I got a phone when somebody—I don't remember who—brought me one weeks, if not months, after Chad's death."

"I had no phone either," Laszlo said. "I ended up back in Norway, while I was recovering. But I was originally in the States for a good nine months, along with everybody else."

"Were you all in the same hospital?"

Laszlo answered, "No. Our injuries were in different stages and needed different specialists. We were split up all over the place. I was actually in England for the first three weeks."

"And I was shipped home. Here to San Diego."

"Actually, no, you weren't," Laszlo said. "That was later. You were in Mount Sinai Hospital."

"That's right. I was sent to San Diego after I came out of the first major bout of surgeries but with many more ahead of me. At the time of Chad's death, I was in San Diego though."

"Yes, you were. And that was a public hospital, not the naval hospital, due to your particular doctor's assignment there. And, even in the Intensive Care Unit, you certainly could have had visitors. You would have had *family* visitation. But only family at that time," Laszlo said. "But that doesn't mean our guy couldn't have walked in as if he was your brother."

Talon's heart still had trouble reacting. "That would be just too unbelievable. So, he blows me up, has my best friend run down, then walks into the hospital, and tells me in person?" He stared at Laszlo. "How did you find out about your father?"

Laszlo frowned. "My brother told me."

"That makes sense. But I didn't have a brother to tell me. So this guy steps forward and tells me instead …"

"I would have told you myself if I could have reached

you," Clary said. "But I didn't have any contact information for you. I found some older phone numbers in Chad's things. But, when I called the numbers, they just went to voice mail."

"Voice mail or just died off?"

"I don't remember." She shrugged. "At the time I tossed away the notes, thinking they were old contact information."

"And they would have been. Even my most recent phone was lost in the accident in Afghanistan."

"I had separate phones for business and certain missions," Laszlo said. "Burner phones that couldn't be traced."

"The only way he would have gotten into the Intensive Care Unit of the hospital was if he had gotten permission."

"And, if he got in, he would have had to show ID, to let somebody know who he was."

"But who'll remember if some relative showed up a year ago?" Talon thought a bit, then, with a smirk, said, "Nurse Ferguson will. She's a dragon lady of a nurse. And she's the one who wrenched me back from the brink of death again. She's also the one who I tried to fight off. She wouldn't let me go." He stared out the living room window, saddened at the tiny mental window he'd opened into his past. Quietly, but with heart, he admitted, "I owe her my life."

"Will she remember you?" Clary asked.

"She would certainly remember me and my downward slide. I'd think so anyway. But I don't know if she'd understand what brought it on."

"Somebody must have," Laszlo said, "because you weren't allowed any access to the outside world after that. When they realized you had no family or friends, surely that must have raised red flags?"

"It sounds like it's time to contact her and see," Talon

said with a look at Laszlo. "We don't have anything better to do this afternoon anyway, do we?"

He grinned. "This is partly what we came here for. If we can find answers, then you know that's what we need to do."

"Wait. I don't want you just taking off and getting answers without keeping me in the loop anymore," Clary demanded. "I might still have parents, but you were always one of my best friends. You were very important to Chad and me. I don't want you walking away, thinking that another eight years is okay before you say hi again. Go do what you have to do but come back here for dinner. We'll barbecue in the backyard. It'll be like old times."

Talon looked at her, knowing this would never be like old times ever again. And maybe that was a good thing. Because, back then, he'd walked away from her. And he knew that, if he ever got another chance, if she'd let him back into her life, he would never walk away a second time.

Talon parked the vehicle in the hospital parking lot and stared through the windshield for a long moment. He lifted his gaze to the huge building towering above them. "You know how badly I *really* don't want to come back here."

Laszlo nodded. "I don't blame you. In this case, it could be made so much worse because of the information we might find out. On the other hand, any information is information we need. Given this asshole's predilection for inflicting pain, I'd seriously listen to whatever that nurse has to say. I don't see how it could *not* have been him. Especially if you don't know how you did hear the information."

"Maybe somebody told me. Maybe it was one of the nurses. Maybe I overheard something. I just don't know."

"And that's why we're here." Laszlo hopped out of the Jeep Wrangler, slammed the door closed, and walked around to the front of the vehicle. "Come on. Let's go. You gotta rip off that Band-Aid and get it over with. We already know she's on duty this afternoon. It's time to ask a few questions. If she doesn't have anything to offer, then we can pick up some steaks and return to your girlfriend's."

That comment jolted Talon out of his thoughts. "Like hell she's my girlfriend," he groaned in a friendly tone.

Laszlo snickered. "Oh, I see, hear, and feel a lot of history between the two of you. That kind of temper doesn't come from nothing."

"I told you that I broke it off with her. She was better off without me. I couldn't be who and what she wanted." He wondered when he'd ever really believe it because he wasn't sure he did even now.

Laszlo didn't reply.

Talon figured that was a good thing. He didn't want to have to punch out his friend for calling Talon a liar. Especially when it was the truth. Talon groaned as they walked up to the double front doors, both of them opening automatically in front of them. "Okay, so time may have changed a few things," he said, "but it's obvious she's moved on. She got married."

"And divorced. Remember that."

"Oh, I remember it," Talon said. "I've had a few relationships in the meantime too."

"More than a few and none of them serious," Laszlo pointed out. "You think we didn't all notice? There was either a big hurt in the background or a big love just waiting to blossom again. Too often it was both."

They approached the front desk and asked to see Nurse Ferguson. The woman smiled and made a couple calls. "She'll be right down."

Talon nodded. He wasn't sure how he felt about it, and he knew she was waiting for them to arrive. He'd already called and asked if she'd give them a few minutes of her time. But it still wouldn't be a terribly comfortable conversation.

They wandered the small front lobby room, noting the various dispenser machines for candy, coffee, and whatnot. He wondered what the world had come to when everything came in packages and boxes and cans.

He shoved his hands in his pockets and stared out the glass window, remembering the last time he'd been here. Thankfully, before he got too far down memory lane, a voice behind him asked, "Talon? Is that you?"

He turned to see the large robust woman who hadn't let him die, even though he'd given her plenty of options to walk away. He grinned. "Hi, Helga. How are you?"

Her face split in a massive grin, showing a mouthful of white pearly teeth. She laughed. "Damn, it's good to see you." She walked over, put her hands on his shoulders, and eyed him critically from head to toe. "And you're looking really good." She stepped back and grinned again. "I am happy to see that. For a while there, I wasn't so sure."

Knowing he'd given her lots of grief, he inclined his head. "For a while I wasn't either. But I do owe you my life many times over."

She shook her head. "We lost you once or twice or came close to it. And I've seen lots of men hell-bent on making sure they didn't survive for one reason or another, but I knew that, if we could just get you to turn that attitude of yours into something more positive, we'd whip the hell out of those injuries, and you'd be back on your feet in no time." She stepped back again and looked at him, noting the hand. He held it out for her to see as he opened and closed the fingers. She nodded. "Looks like it worked."

"Outside of a few setbacks," he said, "it did work. And I owe you an apology for being such a shitty patient."

She chuckled. "Now if all my patients would come back and say that, it would make my day so much better." She turned to look at Laszlo and smiled. She held out her hand. "Helga Ferguson. Do I know you?"

Laszlo shook his head. "No. And I guess that's my loss. I was in the same accident as Talon."

Her sharp eyes missed nothing as she studied his stance and face. "You obviously recovered in a different hospital."

"Several of them," he said cheerfully. "I was never as cranky as Talon."

"It'd be hard to be as cranky as him," she said on a laugh. "Some men make good patients, and then there's you military guys. Generally you're just capital bastards when you're flat on your backs, immobile and helpless. But understanding the whys and hows makes it a lot easier for us to deal with you. And, at some point, you're back on your feet, strong as ever. And it's always really good to see such progress. As delighted as I am to see you came for a visit, I'm sure there was a reason behind it because almost nobody comes back here voluntarily."

"That's too bad," Talon said quietly. And he realized something he should have done a long time ago. "Because I do owe you my thanks. There were some days when I was pretty down. I didn't think my life was worth living, and you never let me wallow."

She shook her head. "Wallowing is not my thing. And normally it's not yours either," she said with more insight than a lot of people had. "So, what brings you here?"

"Remember when I heard the news about my best friend

dying in an accident?"

She winced. "Yeah, we almost lost you there again. Not only did you fight us so bad but we had to knock you out. Then you didn't want to come back to the surface again. You also had reinjured several of your wounds, tore out a bunch of stitches, and caused general mayhem. Why? What about it?"

"Any idea how I found out that news?"

She stopped, frowned, tilting her head as she studied his face. "I'm not sure I do. Why?"

"Because that friend of mine we now know was murdered," he said, having difficulty getting the words out. "And now there is a question as to how I might have found out about his accident. I had no cell phone. I had no access to laptops or any electronic device. At the time I was still recovering, not capable of handling most of those things. I have no family, so nobody was, as I believe, allowed in to see me ..." He let his voice trail off as she understood the problem.

"It could have been a nurse who told you," she said cautiously. "Although I would have had that person handing in her resignation if she'd done that. You were very unstable. Your condition was still critical. Something like that could have killed you."

"And that's why we're wondering if it was done deliberately," Laszlo said. "As in potentially the man who murdered his friend wanting Talon to know his friend had died. Because what we're learning is, with everything that's happened, somebody is trying to inflict maximum emotional and psychological pain upon each of us who survived the initial land mine."

They followed her to her office. As she walked in, she

motioned to two chairs. "Sit down."

They both took a seat. Talon looked around. "Did you have an office when I was here?"

"No, I've recently taken a slight promotion. A little less patient time, a little more paper time, and maybe a little less stress." She shrugged. "But the jury's out on that last one."

He nodded in understanding. "As long as you're happy."

"That's the bottom line," she admitted, her gaze on the monitor as her fingers clicked away on the keyboard. "Okay, I have your file. Give me a minute while I quickly go through this."

He could hear the occasional clicks as she flicked through page after page after page. He knew the file, if printed out, would be thick. His recovery had not been the easiest. On the other hand, he *had* recovered. So, given the condition he'd been in at the time, maybe it was a miracle after all.

She stopped on a page and read out loud. "It says here you received bad news." She leaned forward slightly. "It says you had a visitor. The visitor disappeared after you crashed. Nobody had a chance to talk to him."

"Any idea who the visitor was?"

"Visitors for the patients in the ICU had to have special permission," she said. "Let me check further. Thankfully all these files are digital now."

Talon sat quietly waiting, but he knew in his gut there wouldn't be any record.

Finally she looked up at him around the monitor. "There's no registered visitor."

"Meaning?" Laszlo asked.

She frowned at him. "Meaning, he didn't check in. He didn't have permission to be here. That *can* happen, but it's rare," she said slowly. "Usually when we don't allow close friends, like a girlfriend, to visit, they often try dubious means to get in to their loved ones. But you were under a pretty close suicide watch at that time."

"So how would someone have gotten in?"

She admitted, "I don't know. In theory, he shouldn't have."

"Unless he really wanted to," Talon said. "And was skilled at getting into places where he didn't belong."

CHAPTER 5

CLARY DID A quick clean-up of the house. She didn't have enough lettuce for a salad, and she was out of potatoes. So she had run out and picked up enough to get through dinner. The men were supposed to bring the steaks, but that didn't mean she expected them to bring everything for a full meal. She decided baked potatoes and a Caesar salad would be ideal. As she considered the temperature outside, she chose to do a potato salad instead. The potatoes were peeled and in the now-boiling water, as she turned around to look at what else might need to be done.

Hearing a sound at the front door, she realized Talon and Laszlo were back already. She turned down the fire under the potatoes and walked out to the front to welcome them. But nobody was there. She opened the door wider and stepped outside. Their vehicle wasn't here; nobody's vehicle was here.

What had she heard? Frowning, she looked around the front yard. On the walkway toward the driveway was a mouse. A dead mouse.

With her heart in her throat, she walked a little closer and gasped. She backed up several steps, then turned and raced inside, slamming the door shut. She leaned against the wood panel, reaching a trembling hand to her forehead. She didn't know what to do. Should the men see that? Or should she just dispose of it so nobody would see it? The trouble was, that wouldn't erase the memory of it from her mind. She doubted anything would do that.

All of the limbs had been cut off the mouse, placed slightly apart from the torso so it was obvious what had been done to it. She could only hope for the poor thing's sake that he had been dead before being mutilated. She pulled out her phone and checked for Talon's and Laszlo's numbers. They had given them to her before they left. Finally she found them. Her fingers trembling, she quickly sent Talon a text. **Where are you, and when are you coming back?**

Going for steaks. Be there in 30 minutes.

Fine.

She debated telling them about the mouse, then realized they would probably cut short their shopping trip and come straight to her home.

She wished she knew if that asshole who had left the mouse was gone. She suspected he was sitting somewhere so he could watch and get a full view of everyone's reaction. Otherwise why do it? Few people like to leave presents and not see what kind of a reaction they got.

She forced herself back to the kitchen to check on the potatoes, but she couldn't help looking around the corners to ensure nobody had slipped into her house. It was just too damn easy, as the men had pointed out. With a door unlocked, a window open, somebody had taken the measure of the security in the house and had let her know how easy it was to enter.

She glanced around but, seeing nothing, walked to the stove. Using a fork, she tested the potatoes, then drained them. When they were dry, she tossed them with Italian salad dressing and popped the whole mess into the fridge to cool. Normally she liked to let the potatoes chill in cold water before she did that, but there was no time, and her mind was too drained at the moment.

She kept checking the time on her cell phone, counting the minutes until the men arrived.

Finally she heard a vehicle. Instead of opening the door, this time she ran to the living room window and peered through the curtains, relieved it was them. Then she opened the door and ran down the porch steps and along the walkway, stopping protectively over the mouse.

As they walked up, talking and joking, Talon took one look at her face and froze. "What's the matter?"

Laszlo walked around to stand beside him, both of them looking at her. She pointed to the mouse at her feet. The men walked closer and dropped to their knees. She heard their sucked-in breaths and saw their hard glances as they exchanged looks.

"Is that a message for you or for me?" she asked in a quavering voice. "Or is that a threat of what he'll do to me?" She watched Talon's jaw work as he tried to come up with an answer that would satisfy her.

And then he shrugged. "Unfortunately it could be many things. I would suspect it's a message for me and Laszlo."

She cried out softly, "Why would anyone do something like that?"

"The friend of ours who died, he was part of our unit, and his nickname was Mouse," Laszlo said. "And this asshole is taunting us with the fact that he killed him. And, in this case, this is what he did to the rest of us. The cut-off limbs are definitely a symbolism of that."

She wrapped her arms around her chest, unaware of a slight keening sound coming from the back of her throat.

Talon motioned for her to go inside. "Come on. Let's get these groceries inside, and we'll come back and clean this up."

But it was almost impossible to move. Finally she came to her senses as he spoke again. "Here. Grab these." He placed a bottle of wine and a set of wineglasses in her hands.

She hurried up the porch steps ahead of him, casting one last look at the poor animal on her sidewalk. Talon wasn't giving her any chance to stop and stare. He nudged her forward, back to the kitchen.

"When did this happen?"

"When I texted you," she said. "At the time I thought I should tell you. I decided to hold off because I didn't know exactly what you were doing and if you needed to finish it."

He didn't say anything, just put down the groceries, and, in an effort to keep her busy, he took the wineglasses from her hands and put them on the kitchen table. "Put the wine in the fridge to chill."

She glanced at it to see a popular California rosé that would be lovely with the steaks. She opened the fridge and froze. She stared at the wine bottle, and tears came to her eyes. It was the wine they always used to drink. She'd learned to love it from her parents. Even Chad had enjoyed it. But to think Talon had remembered … Not wanting to make too much of it and not wanting him to see her reaction, she made room for it in the fridge, then reached for the rest of the groceries he'd bought. "Why so many groceries?"

"Because we're staying here tonight," he said, his tone implacable.

She turned in outrage to see him waiting for her to argue. But what was the point? If nothing else, seeing the mouse outside had convinced her that this asshole could come here anytime he wanted to.

"What if it's you that's bringing him here?"

"I wasn't here a month ago, was I?"

She had no answer for that. She slammed the fridge shut and handed him a cutting board.

He took it from her hands, opened the steaks, laid them down, trimmed off the edges, and, with a bunch of ingredients he'd bought, mixed up a dry rub and coated one side. She was fascinated to see him work with such skill.

"When did you learn to cook?"

"I took it up as a hobby after my accident," he said quietly. "I've always appreciated good food. But I wasn't about to go out in public to eat, so it seemed like a good idea that I learn."

She marveled at the change in him. He did so much with his left hand that she couldn't even imagine could be done. It was very mechanical. He could easily grab a knife, pick up a salt shaker, even hold the meat. She imagined it would be a pain to clean, but he seemed very adept at it.

"You're good with the hand."

"I am now. In my case, it's not just my hand that's missing."

She frowned.

He pulled his shirt-sleeve flat to show the bulge in his arm where it shifted from flesh to metal. "In the accident, one of the pieces of metal completely sheared off my arm," he said. "One of the other guys is missing the arm a little bit lower down, just under the elbow whereas I lost mine just above."

"Isn't stuff like that expensive?"

"It is. One of our guys found an incredible prosthetic designer in Santa Fe. It's one of the reasons most of us settled there. Because she's been working on our prosthetics, we have so many visits to get properly fitted. She designed products just for us." He glanced down at his foot. "She just brought me in a blade runner model, so I could go back to jogging a whole lot easier." He glanced up at Clary's face. "I don't know if you remember, but I always loved to run."

She nodded. "We used to run in the morning together."

"Do you still?" There was curiosity in his voice, as if he really wanted to know.

"Yes, but not as much as I should," she replied. "I used to run from my demons after Chad was killed, but it was more a necessity than an enjoyment."

"I understand that feeling. Most of us are doing the same at various times."

She stared, fascinated at his prosthetic fingers. "Does it hurt?"

He shook his head. "No, not now. And as I've grown more adept with it, it's much easier. The pain was in the frustration to begin with. I wanted my arm back, a hand that followed my commands instantly, fingers that would do what I could have done before. And that won't happen."

"They're doing hand transplants," she said impulsively. "But I don't know about whole arms."

He nodded. "I know about the hand transplants. And, if something like that was ever a possibility, it's something I would consider. But I don't think the science is quite there yet. It would be a dream though." He turned and handed her the board. "These are ready for the barbecue, but it would be good if we could let them marinate for a good twenty minutes to an hour."

She took the board from him and carried it to the counter. "The potato salad will need that long anyway."

"Potato salad, yum," Laszlo said. Coming inside, he walked into the kitchen and scrubbed his hands thoroughly.

He must have removed the poor chopped-up mouse from the walkway. "I don't suppose the mouse left a suicide note or the killer left a note to say, *Hey, it's me*, and signed his name?" she asked in a half-joking tone of voice.

Laszlo shook his head. "Wouldn't it be nice if killers did that? Most of the time they just torment their victims and carry on."

There wasn't much she could say to that.

Laszlo finally finished scrubbing his hands, turned with his hands up in the air, looking for a towel.

She got him a paper towel. After she showed him the garbage can, he turned around, leaning against the counter. "Now tell us exactly what you heard."

Surprised, she said, "I didn't really hear anything."

The two men waited.

"Okay. Fine. I thought I heard a noise, like you guys coming back. I walked to the front door, opened it, but it wasn't you. I didn't see anyone, so I stepped out on the front step. There were no vehicles. I looked around. Nobody was there. Then I saw something on the sidewalk. I walked toward it to take a closer look, then backed up and immediately came inside. That's when I texted you." She waited. She was pretty sure they wouldn't like that answer. As they straightened and both stared at her, she rushed to add, "What else was I supposed to do? Why wasn't I supposed to go out there? I mean, you hear somebody at your door, you go to your door."

"That's true," Talon said. "So you won't be answering your door for the next few days."

"Why not?"

"Because he needs to know you're not alone."

She frowned, not understanding what difference it would make. "He's probably here now because you've arrived," she accused. "It's not me that he gives a damn about. It's you."

Talon nodded. "That's right. It's me who he cares about. It's me who he wants to hurt," he emphasized. "And, therefore, he cares about you."

She laughed, but there was no humor behind it. "Then he doesn't understand you very well, does he?"

"Or he understands you very well," Laszlo said to Talon.

Laszlo always seemed to be running interference between the two of them. She appreciated his presence. He was the oil on troubled wheels at the moment. But he was still wrong.

"If this guy knew anything, he'd realize there's no love lost between the two of us. You really cared about my brother but not about me, so, if I get killed off, it won't hurt as much." She couldn't seem to leave it alone. She glared, jutting her chin out toward Talon. "Isn't that right?"

He gave her a lazy smile. "Of course not. I love you now as much as I always have."

But the flippant tone of his voice pissed her right off. "And that would be exactly zero," she snapped. And once again the heavy silence descended on the kitchen.

HE KNEW HE deserved that. But it wasn't the truth. One didn't share as many years together as he had had with Clary and her brother, Chad, without loving them. And he did love them. He was afraid he was still in love with Clary. The fact that it could even be possible was a stunning admission on his part. He knew Laszlo was hoping for something along that line, but Talon swore he'd taken those feelings, ripped them out of his heart, and stomped on them, so he wouldn't feel such pain again.

But apparently, somehow, it still dwelled within him. And that was not good. To be exposed like that was to have a weakness. And he realized that was exactly what this killer wanted. *He was poking and prodding at Talon's weakness.* And the serial killer would have no problem doing to Clary what he had done to that mouse. And Talon couldn't afford to have that happen. Not only because she was the woman of his past but because she was also Chad's sister. And Talon owed his best friend at least to protect his sister while Talon was here. He hadn't been able to help Chad, so Talon *must* help Clary.

He turned around, completely ignoring her, cleaned up the mess on the table, and walked to the garbage. It was almost full, so he pulled out and tied up the bag, and, without another word, walked past her to the front door, opened it, and headed toward the garbage bins.

As he stepped outside, he took a good look around. He noted the two SUVs across the road, the large F-250 parked in front of the neighbors to the left, and a couple small cars parked on the road, as if they belonged to guests or additional vehicles to the houses. Nobody was in any of the vehicles that he could see. Talon then turned slowly, letting his gaze roam. He'd perfected the art of seeing without actually staring.

He turned and walked slowly toward the house. He deliberately emphasized a limp. He wanted whoever was watching, and definitely someone in particular that was watching, to think he was injured and weaker than they expected. Limps didn't always mean that. As Talon accentuated his sore lower back by rubbing it and wincing, he figured that was about all he could do for the moment, especially since he was steps away from the house.

But, if their serial killer or his associate or hired gun thought Talon wasn't as strong as expected, it would make the killer act foolhardy. And Talon wanted this asshole to be more than foolhardy. Talon wanted this guy to be completely arrogant and to think he didn't need to prepare. Somewhere, somehow, this had to end. Talon's mind even now reached for suspects. And he was coming up empty. It made him angry.

He walked into the kitchen after slamming the front door. "Laszlo, how many people actually know the details about your family?"

Laszlo looked up at him from the kitchen table. "Not many. You guys. That's the extent of it."

Talon sat down on a chair beside him. "Same here. Without any family, there was just Chad and Clary for a long time."

"And then there was just Chad," Clary added snappishly.

Talon ignored her again. She was a bit of a temper pot, and he could live with that. She would have to get over her anger though, because he wasn't leaving. Not until they figured out what was going on.

"We also have to remember," Laszlo said quietly, "this guy has no problem hiring others to do his dirty work. So even though somebody was stalking Clary before and then killed Chad, it doesn't mean this particular guy is the mastermind. It just means, another man could have been hired."

Clary said, "So you're saying the guy I sketched might

not be the same man around here now?" She drummed her fingers on the table. "That actually makes sense. I was thinking my neighbor was looking at me rather creepily the other day."

"Which neighbor?" the men asked in unison.

She sat back, raising an eyebrow at them. "Lots of men look at me in a creepy way," she snapped. "You can't just go jump on all of them."

"We don't have to jump on them," Talon said. "Just lean on them."

But his tone of voice left her no doubt about what he would really do.

"What about security cameras?" Laszlo asked her.

"I don't have any."

"What about at your parents' house?" Laszlo asked.

She stopped, looked at him wide-eyed. "Yes. Actually, yes."

They hopped to their feet.

She snatched the keys to her parents' house. "Let's go take a look."

As she went toward the front door, Talon leaned forward, stepping in front of her, opening the door for her. He held her back slightly and stepped out to take a quick look. Then he reached back with his good hand, holding it out for her. She stared at it, then brushed past.

He rolled his eyes as she swept away and whispered, "Always so stubborn."

"Just not a doormat," she snapped back.

"Being a lady is being a doormat?"

Her back stiffened, and he realized she'd taken it as an insult. He hadn't meant it that way. But they used to hold hands all the time. Obviously she had no intention of returning to that. Also he used to call her *his lady* all the time.

She shot him a hard look. “Being independent does not mean I’m not a lady.”

He frowned, wondering where this rough edge came from. “Did your husband not appreciate independence?”

“No, he didn’t. He wanted somebody to look after him. But that wasn’t me.”

“So why did you marry him?” He really wanted to know the answer to that.

She tossed him a look as they crossed a small grass strip between the two driveways. “Because it was comfortable.”

That shut him up. That made no sense to him. She was a beautiful, attractive, smart young woman. He glanced at his feet as they continued to the house next door while keeping his peripheral vision on his surroundings.

Surely somebody out there set her nerves on fire. Wasn’t passion better than comfort? He had to ask himself about that too because he wasn’t sure. He’d had lots of passion with Clary, but there’d been nothing left of their relationship at the end of the day.

That was probably why he didn’t allow himself to have any emotions after their breakup. He hadn’t wanted a serious relationship when he was in the military. Since he’d been out of the dating scene for the two years after the land mine accident, it might be time to reconsider relationships again. But, even overcoming his depression issues and then his physical issues, including adapting expertly to his prosthetics, all those successes didn’t add up to be enough. He no longer felt he was in a position to offer a woman the same things he could have before.

Apparently Badger and Erick didn’t have that problem—Cade as well. Maybe Talon would get to that point himself. But, at the moment, he wasn't feeling too confident.

She unlocked the door, and they walked into her parents' house. Talon smiled, as it was like stepping back in time. It was still decorated from the 1970s when they'd bought it. "Do they still live here?"

"They come for about a week every year," she admitted. "But that's it."

"Have they even talked about selling?"

"All the time since Chad passed." She shook her head and winced. "I don't need two houses, so, if they ever run out of money for their research, this will be the next thing to go."

"How do you feel about that?"

"Before I would have been heartbroken. But with Chad gone now …" She shrugged. "Maybe it's not the place I need to be either."

"But all your family memories are here," Laszlo said, standing at her side.

She turned to look at him. "The memories are in my heart. I don't need a physical location to remind me of what I love."

Laszlo shot Talon a look and a raised eyebrow.

Talon shrugged irritably. There wasn't anything he could say to that. But it was true. And he was glad she was at least settled enough over Chad's death to realize she didn't need to cling to his things. Chad wouldn't have wanted her to suffer. He would have wanted her to go on and to have a happy, fulfilling life. It was the same thing Chad would have wanted for Talon.

The house had a musty smell, as if the windows hadn't been opened for a long time. "How often do you come over here?"

"Not very often," she answered. "I collect the mail but take it to my place. I handle the bills, pay the taxes, pay the utilities. Most of the time everything's turned off anyway."

"Not the power?"

"No, the security system is connected, as are the exterior lights. I needed those on, so I had to keep the power live. But it's an empty house. There's really not a whole lot I can do to make it look lived in. Most people on the block know it's my parents' house, so I don't expect any trouble from them. If anybody saw the furnishings—well, unless you were a 1970s' fan—there's really not much here worth stealing."

He glanced around the living room and realized there were no electronics—no TVs, no digital anything, just like when he used to visit.

"Did they not watch TV?" Laszlo asked.

"No, they were huge proponents against it. They do love their laptops for their work though. They are very connected to the world. But the house is old and just getting older."

"It's kind of sad," Talon murmured.

They walked through the kitchen and into the back room where the security camera monitors were.

She pointed at the equipment. "Because they're gone all the time, they did set this up. It's not really connected to a security system, but it has its own cameras, so they can see what happens inside the house. For a long time, they carried an app on their laptop that let them connect to the routers here, so they could check in on the camera feeds. I guess, by rights, I could set that up at my home too."

In front of them was a small security system, and, indeed, there was a laptop dedicated to it. It was split in four screens that showed the four cameras. She sat down, backed up the video feed to about a half hour before she found the mouse. Then she hit Play.

They sat back and watched all four cameras to see who had left the gift. As it got closer to the time, two of the cameras continued to play normally, but, all of a sudden, something blocked the view of the other two.

"So he blocked the cameras so nobody can see. Then goes about his business." Laszlo was pissed. "I expected it, but there was almost the hope that he'd forget about the neighbors' cameras." Except, as she had said, everybody knew it was her parents' house. "Okay, so we can't tell anything from this house's point of view. What about other neighbors? Anybody else have any cameras?"

They wandered back outside again, and she locked up the house. As Talon stood there, he checked the various nearby houses for security systems, and, sure enough, there was one across the road. With Laszlo and Clary at his side, they walked to the neighbors. He asked Clary, "Do you know who lives here?"

"The Farnsworths. They also travel a lot."

They knocked on the door, and a sixty-something-year-old man answered.

He saw Clary and smiled. "Clary, what can I do for you?"

"I was wondering if you could check your security system from about an hour and a half ago. Somebody left a mouse on my pavement, and I wanted to see if it was something to be worried about."

"Oh dear. It was probably just the neighborhood kids, but, yes, let's go give that a check."

They followed him inside at his insistence. He walked over to take a look.

In direct contrast to Clary's parents' house, this one was completely stocked with electronics.

"Shortwave radio?" Laszlo asked in surprise.

Farnsworth turned and looked at him in delight. "Yes. I'm a bit of a geek," he admitted. "I keep the cameras here." He pointed to four monitors dedicated to the system.

They noticed he also had access for games. Laszlo chuckled. "Now that's a nice setup."

Mr. Farnsworth nodded. "Let me just click into the security system and see what pops up."

He brought up four cameras, the same as Clary's parents' house. Within minutes, he had it backed up to the needed time period, and they could see what had been going on. They watched for a good five minutes, then a small car pulled up. It was a blue Audi. The driver had parked almost on her parents' driveway and got out. He was a young man, maybe early twenties, and he carried a paper bag in one hand and a couple towels in his other. He snuck up under the security camera and tossed the first towel over the lens, then repeated it for the other camera at the front of the house. Then he measured off his steps as if he'd been given explicit instructions as to where to place the mouse, all the while keeping his face turned away from the cameras. Then he gently opened the bag, dumped out its contents, rearranged something on the pavement, and then backed up, keeping the bag with him, got in his vehicle, and left.

Clary sat back. "Wow. Well, that was the guy."

Talon leaned forward. "Would any of your cameras catch that license plate?"

The man flicked through one of the other cameras, brought the feed to when the car pulled up, and enlarged it ever-so-slightly. "We can't get all of it, but there's the first letters and numbers."

Laszlo wrote them down to research later.

They thanked Mr. Farnsworth, and walked back to

Clary's house in complete silence.

Settled now at the kitchen table, Clary asked, "Did you guys recognize him?"

"I didn't," Laszlo said. "Talon, did you?"

"No, but we should also check with Faith to see if she recognizes this man as the one who came to her door. He fits the general description she gave us, but to have her ID this photo would be huge." He was already sending the image to Faith. "Have to remember, she was so excited about Elizabeth calling her she didn't take much notice of him."

"Still, let's see what she says." Laszlo frowned, shook his head. "I guess he would have flown here. Otherwise that'd be a lot of driving if it's the same guy, first appearing at Faith's apartment back in Santa Fe and now here at Clary's home in San Diego," Laszlo said as Talon's phone beeped.

"It's Faith. She says, possibly but she can't be sure. The guy at her door had a different hat and facial hair."

The two men looked at each other. "Not helpful," Laszlo said. "But doesn't take him out of the running."

"It'd be about a twelve-hour drive one way. That'd be a long trip to do in one day by himself, but, if he had a partner, they could swap out the driving when one got tired. Regardless the trip could easily be done in two days."

At that Laszlo nodded. "True enough."

They turned to look at Clary sitting quietly at the kitchen table, as if lost in thought.

Talon remembered her question and sat down beside her. "Do you recognize him?"

She shook her head. "But there was just something about him." She got up, walked to the living room, grabbed her sketchbooks, flipped to the page where the two men were at the table in the coffee shop and tapped the photo. "I think it's him."

CHAPTER 6

CLARY STARED AT the sketch she had drawn, trying to figure out what she had seen in that camera feed versus what she saw here. "In the camera he looked younger." She raised her eyes. "How would he have done that?"

"His clothing, for one. He tugged on a baseball cap, a muscle shirt, and a pair of jeans to drop off the mouse. I don't know what he wore in the restaurant, but, depending on his attire, it often ages a person. And the hair. In the camera he had very long hair."

She nodded. "So you think he's using disguises?"

"I would imagine so."

Talon got up, walked to the double French doors, and stepped out.

She followed him. "If you're hungry, we can light the barbecue, and I'll get the rest of the food ready."

But he was wandering around the backyard.

She watched as he checked all the corners, as if to determine how secure her property was. She glanced over at Laszlo standing on the veranda, his arms crossed over his chest as he watched his friend. "Is he always like this?"

"Always," he answered. "He doesn't sleep well at night either."

She winced but could understand that. It wasn't hard to imagine that more than a few demons ruined his world on a regular basis. "You weren't as badly injured?"

"I was, yes. You just can't see most of the scars. I lost my spleen and a kidney, for starters. I have rods in my spine, an artificial hip, a missing foot, and a badly burned left hand. I even have a metal plate in my neck, supporting the weight of my head."

She stared at him. "Really?"

"Really. None of us came out of that accident easily. We'll have a lifetime of issues, a lifetime of adaptations. Even psychological issues from all this as well."

Something in his tone had her feeling like it was safe to ask her next question. "Are you warning me off of him?"

He chuckled. "If I could do that, you aren't the woman I thought you were."

"You don't know who I am," she said with spirit.

"No, I don't. But I do know him. And anybody who takes him on won't have an easy time of it. We all have nightmares, reliving the land mine explosion. We all are haunted about losing Mouse, just a kid, fresh in the navy, someone we looked after for a year, and yet still couldn't prevent his death. *Survivor's guilt,* they call it. We're dealing with that loss by finding out who the hell did this to all of us. In a way, this mission is therapeutic. But it doesn't solve our physical problems. We have to take medications. We have to see doctors. We have to go for follow-up visits. We have to get our prosthetics checked out on a regular basis. There are constant tweaks."

"Granted, your injuries are on a larger scale, but, not to diminish the extent of the damage done to your body, anybody with even a single health issue has to take care of many similar things." She watched as he slid her a sideways glance. "Chad was a type 2 diabetic—thankfully adult onset so he could still be a firefighter. There were lots of adjustments that needed to be made for him."

She watched the surprise in Laszlo's eyes, but then he gave her a quick nod, as if he understood all that was inherent in Chad's life.

"He never complained. He often worried about not having enough insulin available as the doctors only wanted to give him prescriptions for ten days in advance."

"I would think that several months would be a given, concerning the issues with diabetes when the blood sugar is not regulated, just as a safety factor," Laszlo said in surprise.

"Sure, but doctors are doctors. They like to make life difficult."

"It sounds like he adapted."

"He did. And that's how I know you and Talon will also." On that note, she turned and headed into the kitchen. She didn't know about Talon and Laszlo, but she was getting hungry. She got an onion and chopped it. Taking out her preboiled eggs, she cut them in small pieces.

Laszlo watched her from the doorway quietly for a moment.

Next she grabbed the marinating potato salad and added the other ingredients. Then she quickly mixed up her favorite dressing to top it off and tossed it all together.

Laszlo stepped inside and then smiled. "Can I help?"

"You can check on the fire in the barbecue," she said, not lifting her eyes from the potato salad.

By the time she was done, the barbecue was ready to cook the steaks. She reached for them, and, turning around with the board in her hands, Talon stepped in and took the board from her. "We'll handle this part."

She rolled her eyes at him. "How very male of you."

He shook his head. "Not at all. You've already done the rest of the work, so we'll do this." He took the steaks outside, and he and Laszlo stood at the barbecue.

Nobody had asked her how she wanted hers cooked.

She thought back to all the times she and Chad and Talon, of course, had had barbecues and realized he probably already knew. She still loved her steaks medium-rare.

There was a nice table outside. She grabbed a washcloth, went out, wiped it down, and then set it for dinner. As she brought out the potato and Caesar salads, she turned to face the men. "Do you want the wine for dinner?"

Talon turned and smiled. "Laszlo can stand here and watch these. I'll open the wine." He followed behind her as they returned to the kitchen.

She opened the box of wineglasses he had brought. "Why did you bring these?"

He glanced at her and frowned. "It's funny, but I assumed you didn't have any."

She stared at him, her eyebrows creasing. "We used to have wine all the time."

"I know. But I broke most of the glasses," he confessed.

The memories slammed through her. He was right. They often broke them. But that was usually because their passion had erupted, and everything around them got scattered. Heat washed over her cheeks. She rolled her neck, as if to get the kinks out, but it was to hide her face, which had to be sporting a full-blown blush if the heat that had gathered there was any indication.

He chuckled. "I see you remember too."

She dared not say anything. She took the wineglasses to the kitchen sink and washed them in very hot water, drying them thoroughly.

As he took out the wine bottle, she put the glasses in the freezer for a moment to chill them. When he had the wine open and looked for the glasses, she retrieved them, and they both stepped out onto the deck again.

It was perfect timing, as Laszlo was just taking the steaks off the grill. She smiled and sat down. "I can't remember when I had a meal like this," she confessed. "I do know it was before Chad's death."

Talon nodded. He lifted his glass and held it up, proposing a toast. "To Chad," he said quietly.

She clinked her glass with his and whispered, "To Chad." In her mind she said, *Well, brother, he's here. And I don't like why he came to see me after all these years, but I'm really glad he did. I hope wherever you are, you're happy. I love you.* She took several bites of her steak. When her mouth was empty, she nodded her head with a slight jerk toward the backyard and asked Talon, "What did you find out there?"

When there was nothing but silence from the other two, she put down her knife and fork. "Look." She crossed her arms on the table and stared at them. "You'll be staying here, so you said. This was about my brother. Now it's about me. But it's all really about you two. So you need to share information with me. I'm part of this sick drama too. I'm not sitting here, in the dark, while you guys make decisions that affect me."

Laszlo took another bite of steak and chewed comfortably. He never said a word.

She glared at him, wondering how and when he decided to step in between her and Talon. Obviously now was not one of those times. *Men. I'll never understand them.* Then she turned her attention to Talon. "What gives?"

He shrugged. "We don't have a whole lot to say." He cut

a piece of steak, but, before he popped it into his mouth, he said, "Somebody did come into my hospital room to tell me about Chad's death. But the hospital has no record of an authorized visitor on file."

"So that means what?"

His laser gaze stared at her as he chewed, then swallowed. "It means that, whoever it was, snuck in."

She sank back in her chair. Her steak no longer looked quite as appealing.

He motioned at her plate with his knife. "Eat up. Enjoy it while it's hot."

"It tasted better a few minutes ago," she said in disgust. Yet she straightened and cut her steak again. "I just can't believe somebody would go to all that trouble in order to tell you the news about my brother, purely hoping it would upset you."

"But it sounds like that is exactly what this guy did," Laszlo said. "And, in case you think it's a lot of trouble, it isn't. I could sneak into any hospital across the country—even one under heavy guard while secret surgery is performed on our president—and not get caught."

She stared at him in wonder. There was no boast in his tone, only a complete acceptance of his skills. "But then surely it's only people with special training who could do that."

Again the two men exchanged glances, and Talon nodded. "Exactly. There's a very good chance whoever is doing this has been well trained, either by our government or somebody else's."

"*Government.* Do you mean navy?"

"It's best if we don't narrow our focus based on too many theories and conjectures. Yet we still must theorize, like we would do to prepare for any mission, any op. The fact that someone—who we call the boss man—knew us, knew our names, knew how to find our families, makes me think navy. But we train with all other military forces. Not only our country but ally countries too."

"But, like you said earlier, this second guy had been well rehearsed or well trained to drop off the mouse. In other words, his boss, the man you seek, could be anybody from anywhere in the world," she exclaimed. She scooped some potato salad onto her plate and took a bite. She let the flavors roll around in her mouth while she thought about what he'd said. "And, of course, after all this time, nobody remembers anybody coming to visit you in the hospital, right? Nobody could describe him? So we can't compare that description to our guy from today?"

"We've only spoken with the nurse who stayed with me a lot. There are a lot of shift changes involved in any hospital, a lot of different staff on any given day, so it's possible somebody would remember him. We haven't tugged that line yet. But most likely he would be an expert at being a chameleon. He would be the kind of person who would slip in, and you would never really have noticed him."

Clary shook her head. "Are you saying your visitor was dressed like a doctor, a nurse, an orderly?"

Laszlo smiled. "That's what I would do." He took a sip of his wine. "Or I'd be a patient in the backless gown, in a wheelchair or maybe on foot dragging along my saline bag, taking a slow spin around the floor under my own power."

"You guys are seriously scary with the way you think."

"Have to be to survive out there," Talon said.

"What about the hospital's cameras?"

"Another line we need to tug. It's possible the cameras

caught our guy from the back, but he'd never let his face get caught on camera," Talon said thoughtfully. "Still, I was in a civilian hospital, as that's where my specialists were, so I wonder what kind of security system they would have."

Laszlo shrugged. "Mason may know somebody."

"In this case, we're probably better off talking to Levi." Talon slowly put down his knife and fork. "Isn't Ice connected to the medical world?"

Laszlo said, "Her father runs a private hospital here."

Talon nodded slowly. "And might just be able to get that kind of information for us." He pulled out his phone and sent a text.

She glanced at him. "Are you texting those people?"

"No, I didn't get the date that this all happened from the nurse. If she can give me the actual date, then maybe I can find somebody who can check the security footage."

"But surely they won't have it for that far back?"

"I have no idea how long any hospital keeps those feeds. But, knowing a little about patients' propensity to sue hospitals, given their deeper pockets, I'd figure they'd keep it all. Who knows when somebody will sue them years afterward? Plus everything is digital now. There's no reason for them not to have it."

She was sorry she'd brought it up. She took several more bites of her food. The meal had been excellent, but it was a little hard to enjoy, given the subject matter.

Just then Talon's phone rang. "It's Erick." He pushed back from the table. "I have to take this," he said, as he stood and hit Talk. "Erick, what's up?"

She watched as he walked across the patio, out of hearing distance, and onto the grass, pacing from left to right in the backyard. She glanced over at Laszlo who was eating as if the phone call meant nothing. "So, are you really hungry, or you're not concerned about the call?"

"Both. Talon will tell me when he gets back. And I might as well enjoy my steak while it's hot."

She glanced over at Talon's plate and realized he'd already eaten most of his. She shrugged, smiled, and finished hers. "Depending on how long he is on that call, we can always throw his back on the grill."

"It won't be that long. He'll tell them about the incident today and maybe get somebody to contact Levi."

"Do you guys know everybody in the industry?" She was amazed at the number of names being tossed around. None of them meant anything to her, but surely a man who owned his own private hospital was somebody worth knowing.

"Nope, just a lot of good ones. But don't forget. All seven of us were in the navy for ten years, but the last five years we were in the same unit. Mouse was just with us that final year. We met a lot of people in that time."

"Did you really do training and war games with the army, marines, air force, etc.?"

He grinned. "Yep, sure did. Some of them were a lot of fun. But, more than that, we did a lot of training overseas and up north. With our own men and with soldiers from other countries. We came in contact with many people."

"And were there a lot who hated you?"

He was just finishing his last piece of steak. He scooped some potato salad onto his plate, then added the Caesar salad. As he chewed, he looked like he was thinking. "That's the problem we keep coming back to. We don't know anybody who hated us like this. We're trying to run down something in Mouse's background. Looking for connections. Motives. Something that would explain this nightmare. Like maybe there was somebody who really hated him—or really loved him and blames us for not being able to protect him."

She sat back. "Interesting issue."

Talon sat down, rejoining them, and attacked his steak in vigorous movements. She watched him take several bites and chew hard and fast. She couldn't decide if he was angry or energized. There was a glint in his eyes, as if he was on to something, but they might not like the answers.

When he finally finished his steak, he did the same as Laszlo had, served himself both potato and Caesar salads. She waited until he finished filling his plate, then asked, "And?"

Surprised, he looked up and studied her face. "And what?"

"You said you had to take that call," she said in exasperation. "The least you could do was share it with us."

He shrugged. "Our friend Badger is doing much better," he said. "But I doubt that means anything to you."

"He was injured in the same truck accident as you, wasn't he?"

Talon nodded. "And he had to go back under the knife recently."

"I'm sorry for him. I'm sure you've all had more than enough of hospitals and surgeries."

"Exactly."

He took several bites of potato salad while she waited for more answers. But it was like pulling teeth. "Did you tell them about our visitor today?" She brought this up, hoping for a different tact.

"Yes. They'll contact Levi and Ice."

It was an unusual name—and unforgettable. Still, from what she'd gleaned, they were also good friends and that meant she was grateful to them for helping Talon out. He'd been alone too long. "When will you know?"

"Not until tomorrow."

"Anybody else have any other leads?"

Talon looked over at Laszlo. "They got into some interesting files in the hit man's laptop."

"From what I saw, he did keep full emails, maps, payment history on every job he ever did."

"Seventeen of them. Erick's already contacted the local detective we worked with the last time. He's very interested in seeing how many cases they can close over this, and he'll contact the necessary authorities who have the open files."

"And yet he was just the paid hit man, correct?" Laszlo asked.

"It appears that way. But Erick is hopeful they can find more information. Geir has taken over looking after John Smith's laptop."

"Geir's a good man," Laszlo said. "So the four of them are there in Santa Fe. Two of us are here. That's six. If we could get a hold of Jager, I'd feel better."

"I know. But he's still dark. Nobody's heard a word from him."

She listened to the back and forth with interest but sat quietly, sipping her wine and finishing her salad. As long as they seemed to forget she was here, they were talking a little more freely. But she knew they were too well-trained to ever let anything slip that was important or could get her in more trouble. She didn't want anything about her brother to be withheld or for them to disappear without her knowing and understanding what had happened. To think her brother had been killed because he was good friends with Talon was a bit much to swallow. But it explained what was happening to her. "Did you send in the sketch I gave you?" she asked

Talon. "Or the photo from the security camera?"

"I did. Both."

"Any reason you're not going to the police?"

Silence on the other side of the table was momentary, then Laszlo said, "We have lots of questions. I'm sure the police would have even more. We want more answers first, before bringing them in. At this point in time, the less the police know, the better."

TALON WATCHED CLARY, knowing she wouldn't like that answer. And, sure enough, her lips pinched together, and her arms crossed over her chest. She had obviously learned to control her temper somewhat, whereas before she would have snapped at somebody for that comment. In a quiet voice he said, "At the moment, they would interfere. We need to get as much information as we can, hand it to them to follow up with, while we carry on looking for more."

"But you do intend on calling the cops at some point?"

They both nodded.

When the relief settled on her face, he realized just how worried she'd been. "We've not gone off the wall or under the radar or rogue or whatever it is they say in the movies. We've always been law-abiding Americans protecting citizens. That hasn't changed."

She nodded, picked up her wineglass, and took a big sip.

He didn't want to tell her all the details he had heard from this latest phone call because some of the hits had been pretty gruesome. At least the instructions had been. The hit man hadn't followed them all to the letter. Apparently one husband had arranged for their John Smith to kill the guy's own wife. But the husband wanted her raped and beaten first. Instead the hit man had shot her between the eyes while she'd been sleeping. Never even knew what hit her.

Talon still didn't like their bearded hit man for what he'd done, but at least he hadn't been following the instructions and causing undue pain in that situation. Just another way for Talon and his unit to know that this guy hadn't been the one they wanted. They were after the boss, the one who handed down the orders for the hits on Chad and the family members of Talon's team.

Not to mention John Smith was dead. It just left a bigger mess for everyone else to clean up. They had gotten no intel from the hired gun before he was shot, so they had no more answers, which was the whole purpose of the boss man ending the hit man's life—if the boss was even the one who had killed Smith. In theory it could be yet another hit man.

But then a guy like Smith would only lie when interrogated. He hadn't gotten to the lying part before he'd died. He'd still been taunting Talon's team at that point.

In the end, what Talon and his team had was so much better. Once they dug deep enough into the hit man's life and deeper into the encryption on his laptop, they would get all the answers they needed—or at least most of them. Particularly when the hit man had been so good at keeping track of everything he did. His laptop had been his electronic photo album of all his hits that he had carried out. Talon would never understand why the bad guys kept evidence that would end up convicting them. It made no sense.

He finished his plate of food and stood, carrying his dishes into the kitchen. He knew there was a dishwasher, but the simple cleaning process involving the hot soapy water was often relaxing for him. As he reached for the dish soap,

Clary took the dishes away from him and loaded them in the dishwasher.

"There's no point in having tools that can do your job if you don't let them," she scolded. "Take the bottle of wine back outside and refill the glasses while I load this."

He stopped and waited until she was done. Laszlo made several trips, bringing in the leftovers. By the time they had the food put away and the dirty dishes loaded, the wine bottle had been emptied into their three glasses. They sat outside in the early evening air. Talon knew Laszlo had more questions and needed to get more information, but there was only so much Talon could say right now.

"How bad do you think this situation is here?" Clary asked.

"As bad as it can get. I don't know who this second man is. I just know his cohort was a serial killer. Seventeen people at last count. I suspect that there's at least one puppet master above all these men, pulling their strings. It's him we're trying to get to."

"*Was* a serial killer? So you're talking about that dead hitman you mentioned earlier?" Clary asked.

"He was shot while we were questioning him back in Santa Fe," Talon said. "We're assuming he was killed by the man who hired him."

"So the boss is taking out his minions one by one?" she asked.

"Exactly," he said.

Clouds were moving in, easing the still substantial heat from the afternoon. But, at the same time, it took away the bright sunshine and seemed to suit the subject matter a little more.

Talon glanced at his watch—it was eight o'clock—and

realized it was later than he thought. They still had their bags in the back of the Wrangler. "We never decided if we should see Mason while we're here," he said to Laszlo.

"No. But I don't want to draw any unwanted attention to him, his team, and their loved ones. It's too hard to keep everyone safe. Particularly if the case blows wide open."

Talon understood. Sometimes it was better to keep relationships a little more distant. It also helped to not have any connection to anybody when they were being hunted. "He's aware that even being involved with us in the past means he's in danger?"

"Yes, I'm sure he's put extra protection on Tesla."

Talon nodded. "I would hate for something to happen to either of them or his team."

"He's got a bunch of his men helping us. They've run all the names we've gathered so far through the database, including Corporal Shipley, John Smith, Ben Chambers even, but they haven't been able to come up with anything helpful," Laszlo said.

Talon glanced at him sharply. "When did you find that out?"

"When I was being conspicuously absent on the front step earlier today."

Talon cast his mind back to when Clary had broken down in tears over the news about her brother. "Did Mason have anything else to say?"

Laszlo shook his head. "Lots of stuff in progress. They're checking through the files, trying to cross-check names, all the accidents. Now that we know three hits were directly caused by this John Smith guy—including the nonfatal hit-and-run on my father—it means five deaths weren't. So we need to know who was responsible for those."

"So John Smith was responsible for the deaths of Cade's sister and my friend Chad, plus injuring your father?"

Laszlo nodded. "It's the others we don't know about."

"Well, maybe if we can catch this second guy here, that'll be another piece of the puzzle."

"I'm just getting tired of the pieces." Laszlo spoke in a hard tone. "I want to know who's above all these guys. He's the one we need to stop."

"Maybe the laptop will give us something."

"A text just came through," Laszlo said, pulling out his phone. He flicked through the message, saying, "Mason has a bunch of names for us." He started reading them off.

Talon listened. "I don't know any of those men. Who are they?"

"They are associated with the dead hit man and potentially on the wrong side of life."

Talon shook his head. "None of the names mean anything to me." He glanced over at Clary. "Did you recognize any of those names?"

She frowned. "Can you read them again?"

Laszlo started at the top and read the seven names again.

She stopped him. "Did you say *John MacArthur*?"

He nodded. "Yes. Why?"

"He approached me about renting my parents' house. But I don't know if it's the same John MacArthur. It's not a terribly unusual name."

"But it's not all that common either. When did he approach you?" Talon asked.

She shrugged. "It doesn't matter as I said no. I never saw him again."

"How long ago?" Laszlo persisted.

She gazed up at the sky, deep in thought. "Five weeks

ago?" She hesitated, as if making a guess. "Over the years, I've asked my parents at odd times if they're willing to rent their house, but they always came back with the same negative answer." She shrugged. "So their beautiful empty house just sits there."

"Did he say why he wanted that house?"

"He was looking for a place to live," she answered. "He didn't appear to have a whole lot of means, so I don't imagine he could pay very much."

"When you say, *not a whole lot of means*, what do you mean?"

"He was on an older bike, just pedaling around. He didn't make me suspicious, but he certainly wasn't respectable looking. His jeans were old and ripped. His sneakers had holes," she joked. "And my parents are very particular about who would be in the house on a good day, and I can't imagine their reaction if they found they had a bum for a renter who didn't have a job and maybe ended up smoking dope all day long in their home."

Talon could understand that. It was tough enough to be in the rental market on both sides of the coin. Finding a good match between the two was always important. "Any other names sound familiar to you?"

She shook her head. "No. That was the only one."

Talon nodded. "Ask Mason for the contact information on John MacArthur, just so we can visit with him and hopefully write him off our list."

"Sure." Laszlo sent a text back. He looked up at Talon. "There should be a whole lot more information coming out of that laptop. I'm really hoping there's a lead of some kind there."

"We can always hope." Talon didn't think anything

would come tonight though. He didn't know how long they would have to stay here, but he didn't want to leave Clary here alone, unprotected. "How's your job going?" he asked her.

She snorted. "Terrible. I've been threatening to leave for the last year. But then I don't know how much of that is the divorce and losing my brother," she admitted. "The lawyers have been okay to work with, but they're a very strange group of human beings."

Laszlo chuckled. "They are indeed. I don't have a whole lot to do with them myself."

"Did one of them handle your divorce?" Talon asked.

She shook her head. "No, none of them handle divorces. They're criminal lawyers."

He frowned. "Interesting. Do you think any of their past clients could be bothering you?"

She looked startled for a moment. "I don't see many of them, so I'm not sure. And why would they go after me?"

"Do the clients come to the office?"

"Sometimes, but honestly the lawyers usually end up going to the police station or to the penitentiaries. Some clients are out on bail but not that many."

"Interesting," Laszlo said. "How did you get a lawyer for your divorce?"

She frowned, her gaze going from one to the other. "What difference does it make?" she asked suspiciously.

"What's the relationship like between you and your ex?"

She crossed her arms over her chest defensively and then crossed her legs too, glaring at them. "It's fine. What are you getting at?"

Laszlo said with a heavy sigh, "Very often with ugly divorces, and especially when a woman is being stalked or in some kind of a trouble, it's caused by the ex-husband. But if you have a good relationship, and you managed to sort out all your differences and split your assets without fighting, then I presume he doesn't care either way."

"Care either way? What do you mean by that?"

"He wouldn't feel like he needed to kill you to keep his money."

She stared at Laszlo. "You think my ex might have been stalking me? Or had someone do it for him?" She shook her head and laughed. "He didn't care enough."

"I thought it was you who didn't care enough," Talon said quietly.

She glared at him. "It's the same thing."

"Did you have assets you had to split? A house you had to sell? Any money? Anything he would object to sharing with you?" Laszlo asked.

She looked from one to the other. "We were only married for four-plus years. In all that time, we didn't even have a house. We lived in an apartment. We didn't have a whole lot of money."

"What about all those years you worked at the law firm?" Talon asked.

"I have a savings account and a 401k, true, but so does he. We kept our money mostly separate."

"So it was an amicable divorce?"

She appeared to consider that for a long moment and then nodded. "Yes. I definitely don't see him as being somebody who would want to take me out of the equation. I honestly think it would be just too much effort. He's pretty well washed his hands of me by now."

Talon kept his thoughts to himself, but he also knew that too often divorces were a whole lot less friendly under the surface than what appeared on the surface. But, if she was right, then her ex-husband had nothing to do with her stalker. Intuitively Talon felt it was still connected to him and his unit but couldn't understand why, well after Chad's death, this person would continue to torment Clary unless it was because of Clary herself. And, if so, was it because of her connection to Talon?

Some of the men in his unit knew about Clary but not everyone. Laszlo did. Geir did. Talon wasn't sure about the others. Maybe they all did by now. He'd forgotten who he had told, who he hadn't, and he knew the guys did a little talking among themselves, but they were all friends, good friends. So sharing happened.

Then he realized that, if anybody had gone into Chad's history, Chad probably had a ton of photos of Talon and Clary together. And, considering Clary was an artist, he knew there would be a lot of photos of the two of them around. Anybody who had decent IT skills wouldn't have had trouble finding them. But why would someone think Talon still cared for Clary after all this time? After all this distance? Hell, she was married to someone else for more than four years.

He finished his wine, collected their empty glasses, and turned to her. "Do you want to show us where we're sleeping?"

Startled, she hopped to her feet. "Sure. I forgot about that."

"If you'd rather," Laszlo said, "we can sleep in your parents' house."

She cast a glance over at the dark house beside hers and shook her head. "No, they're pretty fussy even about that."

Laszlo looked at Talon with surprise.

He shrugged. "They're definitely different. They're very much into their research, and this is kind of like a bolt-hole for them but only them. And they want it available at all times."

"I'm not even sure it's that anymore," Clary said. "They're so into what they do that I don't think this is anything other than an asset that, at one point in time, they may be forced to sell in order to keep doing their research work. An asset they don't want anybody to touch. They do all the maintenance on it as required, but that's it."

"Did they come back for Chad's funeral?"

Her shoulders stiffened. "They did, and they left the next day."

He couldn't stop the wince that crossed his face. His heart hurt for her. She'd been all alone. He hadn't even been able to come himself. "I'm sorry. That's not something you should have gone through on your own."

"No, nobody should," she said quietly. "I had girlfriends. Chad was helping me through the breakup of my marriage, then he died, and my failed marriage took second place. I was heartbroken over Chad's death. It just blindsided me, you know?" She glanced at him.

He nodded. "Any accident that takes somebody we love from us suddenly is devastating. In Chad's case, he was so full of life. It seems an even bigger crime to take someone like that."

She nodded and led the way upstairs. "There're two spare bedrooms up here."

Laszlo asked, "Where's your room?"

As they entered the hallway, she said, "I'm in the master at the far end. That was Chad's room."

"He was looking into this stalker of yours, right? Do you

still have Chad's laptop? His cell phone? Any of his notes? Do you know what he did in order to track this man down?" Talon asked suddenly. How could he have forgotten Chad was looking into that? It was a lead they couldn't afford to ignore.

She nodded. Instead of going to her room, she went to the hall closet and pulled out from the bottom space several banker's boxes. "All his paperwork is in here. I didn't know what to do with it."

The two men looked at the boxes. Laszlo asked, "Would you mind if we go through it all?"

She shook her head. "Feel free. But again, you have to share what you find with me."

"Agreed."

Each of the men grabbed a box, and she led them to the first spare bedroom, then pointed out the second. "There's a bathroom you both share between the rooms," she said.

They nodded. "In that case we'll say *good night* after we grab our bags from the car, and we'll start doing some research on what's in these boxes."

She frowned, indecision on her face, and then shrugged. "That's fine. I'll go to my room. I brought home some work—drafting pleadings for my bosses—that I need to catch up on too."

They walked into the room Talon would sleep in. Laszlo dropped his box on the bed. "I'll go out to the Jeep and grab our bags." He disappeared out the bedroom door.

Talon put down his box, taking off the lid. There was a laptop, tablet, and a cell phone. He found more cell phones as he kept going through the box, plus files, a flash drive, and what looked like several external hard drives. There was a lot to go through. Chad was a good man. If he'd gone looking for someone who'd been bothering his sister, he'd have been thorough.

Talon glanced up to see Clary still standing in the doorway. He frowned. "Is there something you want?"

She shrugged. "It's just so weird to see you."

He sat down on the bed. "Hopefully it's not a negative to see me."

"No, and I certainly feel much better knowing why you didn't come to the funeral. It also makes me happy to know Chad did have contact with you all these years. I know he was worried about you at one time, but he never really explained why."

Talon filed away that bit of information. Chad had always been very protective of his sister, and, after Talon and Clary had split, Chad gave Talon only the basics of her life. "He told me very little about your life," he admitted. "He was always protecting the two of us."

She nodded. "Maybe that's one of the reasons why losing him was so hard. He'd always been that big brother protector in my world. Afterward it just seemed like I was so alone."

"I'm sorry. There was nothing I could do at the time."

She nodded. "I understand that now," she said honestly. "I'm not sure you would have come even if you could have. You were very much into your own world back then."

He smiled. "My years in the navy were important to me."

"Obviously. You left me for them," she snapped.

He sighed. "I left you because you wouldn't let me have both. You're the one who gave me the ultimatum—you or the navy—and I had to go to the navy. I really wanted to have you as well, but that wasn't enough for you." He tried so hard to keep his voice neutral, but it was hard, almost impossible, to keep the note of pain out of his words, his tone. "But it was a long time ago. We can be friends. We don't have to still be broken lovers."

She snorted. "Since I've already married and divorced, that lover aspect was a long time ago."

But still she didn't leave. He waited, wondering if there was anything he could say to help bridge the gap. "I am sorry I didn't keep in closer contact. At the time, I was hurt and angry, and it seemed like a clean break was the best way."

Moodily she stared around the room. "And I buried myself in my work and my friends, went through a couple relationships before I hooked up with my husband. But I never forgot you."

"I don't think any of us ever forgets our relationships. I buried myself in work and kept in touch with Chad. I was determined to not lose him too. You two were the only family I had."

She winced. "And now we've both lost Chad."

"But we don't have to lose each other. Nobody can step into Chad's role in either of our lives. In your case, it hurts even more. I understand how close you two were and for many, many years before I showed up. I have a lot of good friends from my unit. It's partly why I didn't need anyone besides Chad. He was my life outside of the military. These men were my life in the service."

"I didn't think you ever needed anybody," she said. "Lord, I was really insecure way back then, wasn't I?"

"You were young. You were very idealistic. You were also adamant about what you wanted. I loved your true independent spirit, and I loved your temper."

She stared at him, her eyebrows rising toward her hairline. "How could anybody have loved that temper?"

"Because it was honest. You never held back, and I could always read you. If I couldn't, I would just get you mad. Then you'd open your mouth and say exactly what you thought. Sometimes it hurt. Sometimes it left everything we had in flames. Then we had to rebuild it. But it was the only way I could get the truth out of you."

She stared at him for a long moment. "Is that why you pricked my temper all the time?"

He chuckled. "Sometimes. You were an enigma to me. I didn't have a whole lot of experience with women, and I didn't understand what you were thinking or how you were reacting. You would clam up and not say anything. Or you'd get up and walk out. Or you'd say everything was fine, but it was obvious that it wasn't fine. If I got you mad, you would start screaming about all the things that bothered you." He shrugged. "I figured that's what guys did. I didn't know how else to get the truth out of you."

She winced. "You're right. I said that *everything was fine* a lot, didn't I? I was afraid you'd leave. I was afraid I'd never see you again because you were joining the navy. That you'd have all these women out in the world, and I was so much less than them, and you would never come back if I wasn't perfect. But I couldn't be perfect, and I didn't want you to always worry, so I was always fine. But, of course, I wasn't fine. You're right. But I didn't know how to communicate what I needed from you."

"At the end you communicated it very well. You said you needed me home every night, and, if I couldn't do that, you weren't interested." His tone turned cold. "That was something I couldn't do. You couldn't accept my career, and you just wanted me to be there every time you yanked my chain."

"It wasn't about yanking your chain," she snapped. "It was about making sure you understood where home was."

"I understood where home was. I just understood I wasn't welcome whenever I had been away and came back. There was a lot of trust I had to have in you too. When I was gone, I was busy looking after the world. I was on extreme training, heavy missions, secret operations. Being dropped all over war-torn countries in the middle of the night, fighting to keep you safe, and the only thing you would have to say to me was I never made it home in time for this or that. And you always complained how you were alone. Yet you had your family here. You had a house. You had Chad, but it wasn't enough. And, if I couldn't come home because my days off were rescheduled, or I was sent overseas, you would lose it. And I could never quite make up for having missed out on some family occasion."

"Are you still doing stuff like that now?"

He snorted. "No, I'm broken, remember?" The conversation was not turning in the direction he wanted it to go. He hated hashing out old problems. If they hadn't worked them out back then, he didn't see what good rehashing it now would do. Eight years was too long for any of them.

"You're not broken, so stop saying that. You've rebuilt yourself bigger, better, stronger than anyone."

"Really? I think you've been reading the internet too much or watching too many superhero movies made from Marvel Comics."

"You were always my hero," she said sadly. "Until you walked away."

"Until you sent me away," he corrected.

She froze for a moment, and then her shoulders sagged.

"Until you didn't choose me."

"I shouldn't have had to."

She lifted her head, looked at him, her gaze harsh and yet full of pain, and nodded. "I know that now."

CHAPTER 7

SHE DIDN'T EXPECT to sleep well, but, when Clary woke the next morning, she was surprised to see it was already 7:00 a.m. She couldn't remember the last time she'd had a solid night of sleep. It was definitely before the breakup of her marriage, before her brother's death, and before all the trauma over the divorce. The divorce in itself was just sad too.

The men were way off, thinking her ex-husband had anything to do with the stalking. He hadn't cared enough at the end, and neither had she. A sad end to a sad marriage. She didn't even know why she'd gone through with it to begin with. Except it was comfortable, and it was what everybody did. And she hadn't necessarily wanted to end up alone. Now she realized being alone was preferable to being part of something that had no joy. That was what was missing in her life for so long—joy. She'd always been so happy when she had been with Talon—before the navy had intervened. In school with him, she had been so optimistic, positive, and full of sunshine. But, after he left, the clouds had moved in. It seemed like they'd stayed that way ever since.

Feeling depressed, she got out of bed and headed for the shower. She didn't know where the men were right now and what hours they kept, but, when they were in the navy, they would have been up early and used to long days. However, after their injuries, she suspected their bodies needed sleep and downtime more than anything. She also remembered she'd given them her brother's boxes last night. If anybody would be able to find anything out from his notes, it would be them.

It had hurt too much to even consider that her brother might have been killed while investigating her stalker. She'd been able to forget about it, as long as it had been a random hit-and-run accident in the parking lot. But still too painful to even contemplate digging through Chad's boxes. She figured, once she'd had a chance to heal, then it would be better. But it didn't seem like she was getting any better.

Now that they'd told her that her brother had been murdered, then, of course, her brother's personal electronics and files needed to be gone through. Thankfully she didn't have to do it alone. Or at all if she could help it. Some things were just too painful, even twelve months later. And other things were even more painful. Still, as long as everybody else could deal with this, then fine.

When she finished her shower, she dressed in jeans and a T-shirt, took her long curly blond hair that was now soaked, wrapped it up in a towel, dried it as well as she could, clipped it back, and let it hang damp down her back. She slipped downstairs, not wanting to wake the men, only to find both of them sitting at the kitchen table, discussing their notes. She frowned. "Did you at least make coffee?"

Both men shook their heads. "We didn't want to take over your house without your permission," Talon said. "I'm happy to make it now though, if you would like."

She shrugged and waved him back down. "I'm here. I might as well make it." She made a pot of coffee, and, while it dripped, she ignored the men, stepped outside, and walked along the garden to see how her flowers were doing. She needed to ask them about anything they may have discovered, but she wasn't sure she was ready for the answers.

When she figured the coffee was ready, she stepped back into the kitchen and closed the door behind her. She poured three cups and carried them to the table. Then she sat down and asked, "So what did you find?"

Both men looked up from their notes. She realized Talon had a notepad in front of him and had jotted things down from Chad's physical research, while Laszlo was doing the same on Chad's laptop, opened right next to Laszlo's laptop, she presumed.

"Was Chad tracking someone specific?" she asked.

"I think so," Talon nodded. "We're still going through a lot of his notes. He was tracking somebody and then added a second man to the list."

"So most likely the two men I saw?"

"There's no way to know that yet. I believe we're a whole lot closer now." Laszlo flipped Chad's laptop around. "Your brother was taking photos of various men. Let's go through these and see if you recognize anyone." Laszlo hit the arrow button and slowly walked through the photographs Chad had taken.

She frowned as she studied them. "I don't recognize anybody."

He stopped when she sucked in her breath.

Her gaze locked on a young man on a bike. "That's the John MacArthur who asked to rent the house." She leaned forward. "At least I think it's him."

"Any chance he would have asked Chad?"

"No, he asked me just a month ago or so."

"Well, Chad's been gone for a year, and he found this person of particular note, so maybe he spoke with him earlier."

She shrugged and sat back, disturbed to think of this man having been around a year ago. "It's possible. Maybe he thought Chad owned it. Chad went over and mowed the lawn all the time."

"Who does that now?"

"I do normally. And sometimes I get a service to come in and do it. They do both houses at the same time then."

"And the other men in these photos?"

She shook her head. "No, I don't know any of them."

Laszlo nodded and flipped the laptop back around so she couldn't see the pictures again.

In the meantime, Talon wrote more notes from the file before him.

"How would you even begin to find out who that person is?"

"Your brother already did the legwork. He found a name, John MacArthur, the same as the man on the bike told you his name was. Whether it's an alias, we don't know yet. But, now that we have it, we can certainly track him down."

"Like I said, it's not an uncommon name. He could be anywhere."

"He could be. But we have ways and means."

She'd heard already how they apparently had a lot of people to help them. And maybe that would be enough to make the difference. She watched as Laszlo flicked through Chad's laptop again, occasionally taking a sip of coffee. By the time she finished her first cup, she was feeling a little more alert. "Did he find anything dangerous? Anything that would have gotten him killed?"

"We're not sure yet. He took extensive notes of all the men he's tracked down and checked up on. He had a friend in the police department run a few license plates of vehicles that came back and forth from outside the city. He was marking down when and how long they were here for. Also he did the same for people at your job, those who came and went."

"My job?"

Talon nodded. "He's got several sheets of notes of vehicles that came and went. But he didn't conclude that any were an issue. Nobody seemed to sit there for any length of time."

It made her head spin to think of her brother being so concerned about her and this stalker that he'd spent days at her office building, checking as she came and went from work, sitting there, following all the moving vehicles. "I do miss him."

"And so you should. He was doing a lot of work to try and keep you safe."

"And what if that got him killed?"

"If it did, it did. It's well past the point of us being able to change things. But let's not have his efforts be in vain," Talon said. "We need to make sure you stay safe. I'm pretty sure he was killed because of me, but, at the same time, it could be that some hit man—or the boss man behind the hit men—will come after you."

"But like you said, he has to have a reason to come back around."

"And we don't know that he doesn't. If he's doing this to make a game of it, he's got to be frustrated that we haven't figured it out yet. However, things are starting to blow wide open now, and I'm sure he's getting into the game a little more. He may come back around, or he may disappear. There's just no way to know."

"Follow the money," she said out loud.

"We'd like to. But we don't have any idea where and how the money is traveling."

"Didn't you say the serial killer you caught in Santa Fe had all his information on his laptop?"

"Yes, and we do have people following the money from there. We don't know yet where from, where to, and what they might find. Obviously we're hoping for a break."

"What you need is to know how he got paid because that's how you'll find out who's the boss man, hiring these hit men." She leaned back. "And that's about the extent of anything I can help with."

The men smiled.

Talon nudged his empty cup toward her. "Not true. You make a mean cup of coffee."

She rolled her eyes. "Because you're working on Chad's case, I'll help but don't take this to mean that I've been delegated the coffee bitch around here." But she was laughing by the time she stood, grabbing all three cups, and filling them again. She had just returned the cups to the table when Talon mumbled at something he was reading.

"What does that mean?" Talon asked. He had a folder in front of him that she didn't recognize. He flipped it open and started going through the paperwork and the images in it.

She pointed toward it after she placed the cups down. "What's that file?"

"The one Chad kept on all your friends and associates."

She froze. "What?"

He looked up guiltily. "I'm sorry. You didn't know?"

She shook her head slowly. "Hell no, I didn't know. What do you mean, on all my friends and associates?"

"Everyone in your life. He'd come to the conclusion that whoever was stalking you was quite possibly somebody very close to you."

She had no idea what to say. It was just a little too much to consider that her brother had been investigating the people closest to her. She held out a hand. "Let me see it." When he hesitated, she narrowed her gaze at him. "Remember how you're supposed to share any of your findings with me?"

He slapped the folder closed and shoved it her way. Then he leaned back and picked up his coffee. But his gaze didn't leave hers.

She frowned at him. "I don't understand why he'd do that."

"Because he was worried about you," Talon said in exasperation. "Honestly I'm damn glad he did. It saved us a lot of time and effort, even if we do nothing else but read his notes and manage to cross off the same people he crossed off. As long as he made logical deductions as to why they weren't valid suspects, then we're good with that too. And he left very detailed notes."

"How would he know to do any of this?" She was amazed as she dropped her gaze to the folder again, hating to even open it.

But she did, especially after making an issue out of it. The folder opened in front of her, she shuffled through the papers, scanning each and every page as she went. Each of the lawyers she worked for, the other three people in the office she worked with, several of her school friends. And, of course, her ex-husband. At that, she pulled out Chad's notes and studied them. She could feel the cold setting in as she realized he'd never liked Jerry in the first place.

She read his notes out loud. "I tried to dissuade Clary from marrying Jerry. But she wouldn't listen. It's obvious they weren't right together, and she wasn't happy. She was hiding behind him. It wouldn't be a good deal. In all the years she was married to him, I don't think that ever changed. However, he doesn't appear to be a suspect at this time. There's a part of me that's really disappointed in that. I'd like to think there was some hard proof he felt something one way or the other. Rage, at least, is the other side of passion. But I don't see that either of them had either emotion in their marriage. Clary shared why they were unhappy, how Jerry felt she wasn't invested, and I agreed with him because I don't think she was. She was still too busy hiding away from her loss. She's never been the same since …" She let her voice peter out as she realized Talon's name was next. Her brother had actually written about Talon after he had left her. She shook her head and slumped back. "This stuff is so old, why would he care?" she murmured.

"He was ensuring every stone was turned to make certain your life wasn't in danger."

She dropped that piece of paper and stared at the folder. It was pretty thick. She flipped through several other sheets. There were pages on her neighbors, even her parents, and their parents' associates at the university. She shook her head. "If I was being stalked, it's much more likely it was a complete stranger than anybody we knew."

"He was being very logical about it. He didn't end up thinking it was anybody who knew you either. But he did take these photos and wondered if any of them had something to do with it. If you notice, at the back of the file, there's a clip of folders. Those are photos, and those are the ones of people who he managed to take off the list. The ones still in this file, which he did cross-reference properly, are the ones he couldn't identify."

She glanced up at Laszlo's laptop. "The ones you pointed out earlier?"

Laszlo nodded. "Those are the seven photos he couldn't take off his list, with one of them being that MacArthur guy."

She slammed the folder shut and shoved it at Talon. "It's incredibly invasive."

"So is an autopsy."

She gave him a horrified look, stood up, and bolted outside again.

"NOT EXACTLY SURE, but I don't think that's the way to win her back," Laszlo murmured.

Talon ignored the look his friend shot him. "I'm not trying to win her back." Yet he stood to watch her from the French doors.

"Why not? It's obvious you still care."

"Doesn't matter if I care or not. I cared last time, and it wasn't enough for her. I'm not the man I was before, even if I no longer have missions of extreme danger," he said sarcastically. "And what I do have, my love now, won't be enough either."

There wasn't a whole lot Laszlo could say to that.

Besides, Talon didn't want him to say anything. Some

things were best left unsaid. He sighed, returned to the table, and sat. He continued to flip through the folder, but he'd already read it once. Talon glanced over at the box. "I wonder how long he'd been working on this."

"Three months, I'd say," Laszlo gave his opinion. "At least by the dates I came up with."

The box Talon had brought down that morning was on the floor beside him. He put the Friends and Associates' folder back and grabbed a small wooden box. He had lifted the lid earlier and had taken a cursory glance, but nothing had meant anything. Now he brought it onto the kitchen table, opened it up, and studied the contents closer this time.

Chad's football ring was here. Plus a couple marbles Talon didn't understand the meaning of and several pictures of Clary and even Talon from when they were much younger. He reached back into the box and pulled out a flash drive. "Did you get a chance to look at this yet?"

Laszlo frowned. "Why don't you get your laptop? I'll stand watch over Clary while you do. You can bring that flash drive up on yours. I've got so much stuff here to go through that I won't get to that for a while."

Talon nodded. "I left it upstairs." He stood, turned, and headed toward the stairs. He glanced outside as he went. Clary stood on the back porch. Instead of her face to the sun, she stared down at her feet, the world around her forgotten. He knew it was a tough time in her life. And, with her absentee parents, that just added to her sense of isolation.

Up in his room, he grabbed his laptop and mouse, returning downstairs. At the kitchen table he plugged in his charger, and, when the laptop had booted, he plugged in the USB. It held many images in a single file. He opened it up and started flicking through them. "I wonder where he got these from."

As he watched the screen change, he realized they were all photos of vehicles. A small Audi. Blue. "He's got tons of pictures of a blue Audi here."

"Any with a license plate?"

"Yes, one with a partial." He flipped his laptop around.

"How many are there?"

Talon checked the file. "Forty-two."

Laszlo lifted his head. "He caught sight of that blue Audi forty-two times?"

Grim-faced, Talon nodded. "Looks like it." He studied the photos closer. "They do appear to be in a different location or from a different angle. Some of these might be the same location." He twisted the laptop around again and showed it to Laszlo.

He noted the image. "What about any damage?"

"Front right fender appears to be dented, and a couple big scratches are along the trunk."

"Send those photos to Levi."

"And Erick," Talon said. He sent the images, asking Erick if there were any further updates. His phone rang a few minutes later, Erick calling him. "Hey, I guess you got my email."

"I did. Somebody on Levi's staff is tracking bank accounts, apparently from overseas."

"Where overseas?"

"Switzerland," Erick said.

"Of course, Switzerland. We don't have any ability to get information from there, do we?"

"No. Some of the money has been routed to England. I was contemplating contacting Jonas out of MI6 to see if he can do any kind of run on it for us."

"Will he though? It's not an official investigation."

"No, it isn't. But the alternative is," Erick continued, "we fly over to England and create mayhem and murder again. Jonas might be happy to get us the information instead."

Talon chuckled. "Who knows? He just might." After a pause, he asked, "You got any other information to add?"

"Since our earlier phone call tonight," Erick continued, "the police have been given the files on all the cases our dead guy was involved in. As some of the crimes were committed in other states, even other countries, they've contacted the FBI to deal with the notifications."

"Good. But you and I both know it's his boss we want," Talon stated.

"What's this about somebody still being after Chad's sister?" Erick asked.

"We're not sure. Apparently somebody was stalking her, and her brother went looking into that issue. When he was killed, she thought it was an accident or could possibly be related to his investigation into her stalker. We now know he was murdered, but, a month ago, she started getting that same creepy feeling of being watched again. She came home, and her door was unlocked. Another time her living room window was open. Things like that. But that all started just a month ago, a long time after Chad's death."

"I wonder if it's the same guy?"

"It can't be our John Smith guy obviously. But it doesn't mean the ringleader doesn't have another hired killer here. Chad has the information in his sister's stalker files, which we're currently going through. He has a lot of photos of a blue Audi."

"The more I think about it, I can't see that our ringleader is the one who came and killed the John Smith gunman in Santa Fe or previously shot at our money man, Warren Watson. Not unless the boss man was desperate, not unless he couldn't hire anybody else to do it."

"Right, but he certainly could have hired somebody in San Diego. Perhaps they were both here. Perhaps this guy moves around a lot."

"No way to know yet, is there?"

CHAPTER 8

SHE DIDN'T EVEN know why she was outside. But a sense of despondency and grief had overwhelmed her when she saw the folders Chad had accumulated on her behalf, when she realized just how much her brother had done to try to keep her safe. Sure, it was invasive. And it was certainly disturbing because he wasn't here to explain it all. But it also showed how much he cared.

She wasn't sure she'd ever felt quite so alone as she did at that moment. The tears were still dripping down her cheeks. She wasn't crying, but she just couldn't stop them from bubbling up at the corner of her eyes. She wiped them away impatiently. It was hardly the time for tears. Two hungry men were in her kitchen, and she didn't even know how long they were staying. She wanted to kick them out and have them take all this news with them. At the same time, she wanted to hold them close and never let them leave.

She wasn't sure she wanted to live in this house anymore. Although it invoked memories of Chad, he wasn't here. And that was such a strange feeling. She was the sole owner now as Chad had left his half to her. It still felt like it was his house. She wondered if living here was the healthiest thing for her. Walking around, touching Chad's things, his furniture, his drapes, his paint on the walls.

Clary could do whatever she wanted to change things.

To make the house hers. Or at least *more* hers. The trouble was, she didn't know what she wanted to do. She had no real inclination to change anything, yet she had no goals to set her sights on either. She was a boat adrift on the waters of life without a sail or oars. When had she gotten so gloomy?

Of course Talon choosing the navy over her had been her first cross to bear. And, yes, now she could clearly see how she had held on to that pain, had nurtured it, had let it fester inside her for almost a decade, which had ultimately led to the hastened death of her ill-fated marriage. Then her parents had pretty much abandoned Chad and Clary to pursue their worldwide research full-time. She shook her head. This was the first time she had ever considered her parents' passion for their research in that context. Clary had really been clueless back then. And then Chad's death … That one event had knocked the wind out of her. For a long time. Probably ever since then.

She knew Talon's reappearance in her life was the first domino to fall, bringing about her fresh eyes, this new insight to view her life for what it was: this destructive rut, pushing everyone away. Except Chad. When Chad had died, she had been thrown such a curve ball that she fell into a horrid tailspin.

Clary pondered what changes she could make to move her off dead center. To add some … life to her life.

She had a job here, which she felt nothing about one way or the other, but she could move anywhere and find another job. It's not like a good paralegal would be unemployed for long. She had a house here, but she could sell it. It wasn't a home—not yet, not really. What she didn't have was her brother …

On that note she gave herself a pep talk so she could get

back into the kitchen without anybody seeing how upset she was. But it would be impossible with Talon and Laszlo. Both men had sharp eyes and seemed to read people easily. She thought about all the work Talon had never told her about, though Chad had hinted at. Secret missions, special ops. "SEALs" had been mentioned more than once.

She could see how Talon would have taken to that life. He'd always been destined for so much more. But, in her heart at the time, she'd been so insecure, so needing a real family, as her biological family had seemed so shattered to her, that she'd given Talon that ultimatum. And she'd regretted it the minute it was out of her mouth. But he'd taken it to heart, and it had been the final blow to an argument they'd had many times.

She took several deep breaths and walked around to the far corner of her property. She shoved her hands in her pockets and let the sun shine down on her face. She had no idea what she would do today. She was partially dependent on the men. They'd come for Chad, to tell her the news. How was she supposed to feel about it? She still didn't know. Because there was no resolution. Now, instead of just needing time to get past the loss, there was an anger, a need to get answers and justice for her brother. And they'd come way too late for any of that to happen.

Maybe that was the part that bothered her the most. If they'd known a year ago, maybe there'd have been a chance to catch this guy—well, the guy who ordered the hired gun. She knew Talon and Laszlo were good at what they did. Obviously they weren't perfect because they'd been in their own accident, despite all their training, all their skills, all that time in the navy. *Thus the term "accident,"* she thought. They weren't talking about that originating incident much, but she was pretty sure they'd said something about a tie-in for all these other murders.

It completely overwhelmed her to consider somebody had set out to systematically kill these men's families and friends. Who had that kind of dedication? Who could possibly hate them that much? For her it all centered around Mouse. As if there might have been a brother or a father or maybe a lover. Somebody who lost the light in their life and wanted others to pay. And all Mouse's team members being damaged from the land mine accident clearly wasn't enough resolution for this person. He—or they, or even she—wanted them to pay on a personal level, like Mouse had.

That the killer had been smart about it and had taken his time and had stretched out his revenge over a couple years said a lot too. For all his hate, he was focused. For all his hate, he was patient. For all his hate, he was persistent. It also said a lot about this man's feelings. The predominant one being *hate*. And how the fullness of it hadn't receded. At all, it seemed.

She was still thinking about it as she walked back into the kitchen and refilled her coffee cup. There was a silence behind her as the men studiously kept their gazes on their laptops. *Of course they wouldn't want to bring up anything that was female-oriented and emotional*, she thought wryly to herself. They were men after all.

She turned to look at them. "Have you started delving into Mouse's life?"

They looked up at her and shook their heads. "Other people are checking into it."

She nodded and explained that particular thought process she'd had outside.

The men were interested in everything she had to say,

and that pleased her. At least they weren't mocking her thoughts or stating she was being foolish. That was something her ex-husband would have done if she said something he didn't like. And yet he hadn't been domineering or controlling in any way. But he'd had very definite ideas of right and wrong. And usually she'd been wrong.

She sat back down at the kitchen table with her coffee and discussed the issue with them a little further. But that was all they could do, discuss. She knew they'd sent off emails and text messages to whomever it was helping them to consider various angles and options, but that was the extent of what they could do. For now. Until they caught a break, until they had a thread to pull, there was just nothing physically happening.

She asked, "What about breakfast?"

The men raised their heads from their work and frowned.

She sighed. "Both of you right now have the same expression on your faces when I say something you don't know how to answer."

The two men exchanged a glance.

"And then you do that. You look at each other, as if the other will have an answer for both of you. Let me rephrase the question. What do you normally eat for breakfast?"

Talon leaned back in his chair. "Anything there is. Neither of us is fussy."

Knowing that was about as clear an answer as she would get, she stood and walked to the fridge. Checking out its contents, she was grateful she'd done a little bit of shopping yesterday and that the men had done some shopping to help out. "There's eggs and bacon," she let them know.

"Looks like we have breakfast then," Laszlo said with a

big smile. "Any chance of bread for toast?"

She pulled out a loaf of brown bread. "Nothing white."

"I don't eat white bread anyway." He nodded toward the loaf in her hand. "That will do fine, thank you."

"How many eggs?" she asked, taking out the bacon and eggs and butter. She turned to look at them. "I have a dozen here, so you can't have more than that." She laughed.

Both men grinned. "Four each as long as you've got them," Laszlo said. "Otherwise two each will be fine."

She contemplated the men. "Do you eat four all the time?"

"He normally eats six," Talon said absentmindedly, his gaze on his laptop. "He's just being polite."

She tried not to show the shock she felt was blazing off her face.

Laszlo chuckled. "I'm a hungry guy."

She rolled her eyes and turned back to the stove. "You can have five each. I'll have two."

"Thank you very much," Laszlo said with quiet emphasis. "Is there anything you'd like me to do to help?"

She smiled. "I'll be fine. You keep working."

She put the bacon into the frying pan, emptying the whole one-pound package. If they ate five eggs each, no way a couple slices of bacon would do it. With the last of the bacon in the pan, she returned to rummage in the fridge for more food. But there was nothing that would feed men with big appetites. She checked out her freezer but didn't find any more bacon or sausage.

She set the table as the bacon slowly simmered. When it was mostly ready, she brought out the second frying pan and started working on the eggs. The trouble was, cooking that many eggs meant she needed two frying pans full at the same time. So, when the bacon was done, she transferred some of the fat to the other pan and cracked eggs until they were all in. Then she turned and announced, "Eggs are on. Clean up so you have space to eat."

Both men put away their papers and laptops. Laszlo got up, grabbed the plates she held out to him. She had the bread in the toaster, and, by the time the eggs were done, the toast was just turning golden. She placed the toast on a plate, putting it on the table, telling the men to butter it as she added more bread to the toaster. Then she dished up the bacon and eggs on more plates, and added them to the table. Bringing over salt and pepper, she added peanut butter and jam to the table.

"Can somebody keep an eye on the toast? Otherwise it'll burn," she cautioned as she sat.

Laszlo nodded, his mouth already full with a bite of toast. For the next few minutes, there was no talk of murders or stalking or men or strange vehicles. Instead it was all about the good food or simply eating it.

When Laszlo brought more toast to the table, she realized she'd completely forgotten about it. She glanced around as she snatched up one of the pieces and asked, "Do I need to put more in?"

Both men shrugged. She sighed and put two more pieces in. She sat back down and said, "That's the end of the bread too."

"No problem," Talon said. "We can stop and pick up more."

She frowned at him. "How long are you staying in town?"

"Until we decide it's safe to leave you."

She didn't know if she should scream at him for assuming she needed him here or to yell for joy because somebody was looking after her again. As an alternative, she just shook her head. "You realize that could be months?"

"Not likely. Probably days. We'll run all the license plates related to the seven unconfirmed individuals. I've sent the photos to some people we know who have facial recognition software to see if anything pops. That'll probably take another day. We're still tracking finances for the other shooter, but, if nothing else happens and nothing else shows up, then there's not a whole lot we can do. However, we will fix your security system here so, if you do get another intruder, you'll be able to check the screens and see who it is and what they're doing."

She wasn't sure about the high-handed way he said they would do stuff but realized upgrading her security system would be a hell of a good idea. If it had already been in place, they'd know who had entered her house and had opened the window. She hated the thought of Talon and Laszlo leaving. She'd never been nervous before, but being alone in this big house, with an empty big house beside her, made her reconsider her options.

"If it's dangerous, I can always go to a friend's place," she suggested. "I do have some girlfriends with spare bedrooms."

"If it comes to that, maybe. But, in the meantime, let's do what we can, see if we can make this work for now."

She nodded. When she was done eating, she waited for the men to finish. By the time the meal was over, she still hadn't heard what their plans were for the day. "With all the stuff you found, is there anything that's actually concrete? Anything that you can go after?"

"The vehicle and that MacArthur guy's face. If we could

find him, I'd like to have a talk with him."

"And the vehicle? What vehicle?"

"You were outside when we found out more about that. On the flash drive we found in your brother's box were a bunch of car photos." He smiled. "But they're all of the same car in various locations."

She stared at them. "A blue Audi?"

He nodded and frowned. "How did you know?"

"I'm the one who took those photos." She looked at the USB and the laptop sitting on the spare chair. "I lost the USB. Where did you find it?"

"In one of Chad's boxes."

She groaned. "That's where it ended up."

"Why did you take them?"

She winced. "Because I thought that car was following me."

"It could easily have been the vehicle that ran down your brother," Talon said gently. "We have to keep an open mind here. No detail is to be dismissed out of hand."

She nodded. "At the time I was too shocked to think about it."

"Was it following you, or was it just … I don't know, a neighbor who shopped in the same places you did?"

"That's one of the reasons I didn't go to the police," she said, twisting her hands, palms up. "It's not like there's an easy answer to any of this stuff."

Talon nodded. "True enough. But, if there's anything else you know or can tell us, then you should let us know now."

"I don't think there's anything else."

"You never mentioned the mail or the phone at all. Have you been getting any threatening letters, any hang-ups, anything odd?" Laszlo asked. He propped his elbows on the table and rested his chin on top of his hands as he stared at her. "Anything at all that might help us?"

"No, nothing. Not many people know my phone number. I keep it that way on purpose."

He nodded. "But people can find out all kinds of information on the internet."

She nodded. "But, no, as far as I remember, I haven't had anything like that. What would it tell him?"

"It's another typical stalker thing. And, other than that, it'll also tell somebody if you're at home."

She shook her head. "No, because it's my cell phone. I always have it with me."

"True. Do you still have a landline in the house?"

She shook her head. "No. Chad never did either."

The two men sat back.

She stood and collected their breakfast dishes. They hopped up and waved her to sit back down again.

Talon said, "We'll clean up. You cooked."

In minutes, they had the dishes in the dishwasher, and the counters wiped.

Talon looked at the empty coffeepot. "Would you mind if I put on another pot?"

She shook her head. "Go for it."

He had a pot brewing in seconds. The guys sat back down again. Talon lifted the box and started going through the rest of the stuff in the bottom. "Did you look at any of this?" he asked her.

"No." She shook her head. "It was all in his office. For the longest time I just left it there. Then I got mad one day and packed it all up so I wouldn't have to deal with looking at it. Except for his bookshelf. It's still there with all his books."

"Did he have a strongbox?"

She shrugged. "Not that I've seen."

"While the coffee is dripping, why don't you show us the bookshelf?"

She got up and led the way to the office on the main floor. As she stepped in, she said, "I would take this over for myself, but, every time I sit here, I think about it being Chad's room. I just feel like it's still his room. So I don't work here, even though I do bring billable work home. Outside of packing up those boxes, I didn't touch anything else."

She watched in amazement as the two men went through the room with knowing eyes and hands. Within seconds they found a wall safe. She gasped as she stared at it. "I had no idea."

"So you don't know what he might have kept in here?"

She shook her head. "No, I don't."

He nodded. "Laszlo, did you find a combination noted in any of the earlier paperwork or maybe there in his desk?"

Laszlo was at the desk, pulling open drawers, all mostly empty. "No. What kind of a lock is it?"

"It's fairly simple. Definitely not something we need a specialist for."

"Well, give it a shot. If you can't get it open, I'll get it."

She watched as Talon put his ear to the lock.

Within two minutes, he had the correct combination dialed in and was opening the door.

"Where did you learn to open safes like that?" she asked in amazement.

"I have a talent for it."

"So why was Laszlo going to try after you?"

"His talent is for bigger safes. I generally do quite well with the little ones." His voice said he was absentmindedly talking as he stared into the interior of the safe. He reached inside and pulled out an envelope. "Underneath the envelope are documents and Chad's passport." He checked the documents and realized they were copies of his and Clary's birth certificates and their parents' wills.

She glanced at the passport and the paperwork and nodded. "This makes sense too. I never could find his passport."

"Well, we're getting somewhere at least." Talon carried the stuff to the desk and put it down, then stared at the brown envelope. It was sealed. He looked at her and said, "Do you mind if I open it?"

She shrugged. "Go ahead. I have no clue what's in it."

He slipped open one end and carefully pulled out the paper from inside. It was a photograph. He gave a silent whistle. "So how sure are you that your ex-husband isn't involved in your stalking?"

She frowned, and he held up the photograph. It was her ex-husband and the guy she had called John MacArthur. The two were standing in front of her parents' house, an envelope between them, as if one were handing it to the other. But each held on to one end of the envelope, so it was hard to discern who was handing it off to the other. She stared at it for a long moment, then slowly collapsed on the chair across from the desk. "But that doesn't make any sense," she protested. "This picture in itself doesn't have any meaning. But to consider it's got something to do with the stalking doesn't make sense either."

"Did you separate from your ex-husband before or after your brother was killed?"

"Several weeks before."

"And you inherited your brother's half of this property, correct?"

She nodded. "Yes, so?"

"If you'd still been together, would Jerry have gotten half of it?"

She frowned and thought about that for a long moment. "I don't know how that law works here in California. When we did settle up our divorce, it was after Chad's death, but we'd separated before."

"Who was your divorce lawyer?"

"One of the men I work with had a friend who took it on."

"And your property from your brother, when did you get that signed over to you?"

She shrugged. "It wasn't immediate. I think maybe five months ago."

"And the divorce, when was it final?"

"Just a couple weeks ago," she said quietly.

Unable to help herself, she got up and ran from the room.

TALON STARED AT the empty doorway. He glanced at Laszlo. "I suppose you think I should go after her?"

"I would. You've opened a big kettle of worms."

He lifted the photo again and checked the back. There was a date written on it. "Five days before his death," he said in a grim tone. He placed the photograph on top of the desk. "I'll go talk to her. Maybe while I'm gone, take a picture of that and send it out and get somebody else's opinion on what we've got going on here."

"How does that have anything to do with our serial killer?"

"I don't know. Maybe we're completely wrong here. Maybe her ex-husband had Chad killed. Maybe our hit man from Santa Fe did the actual killing of Chad. But maybe we had the person who hired him completely wrong. Send Erick the name of her ex-husband and see if we can get any more information off that damn John Smith laptop, especially in connection with Chad and Jerry. I really don't need this extra wrinkle right now," he snapped.

He spun on his heels and headed after Clary. He found no sign of her on the main floor. He checked outside, then headed upstairs to her room. He stood outside the master bedroom and could hear her crying inside. He didn't bother knocking. He turned the doorknob and stepped in. She'd flung herself across the bed, bawling heavily. He couldn't blame her. He walked over to the side of the bed, lay down gently, and pulled her into his arms. He felt her give a start of surprise as she lifted her head and stared at him but came willingly, throwing herself into his arms, holding him close.

Just like before, he held her and waited for the storm to abate. "We don't know for sure your ex-husband had anything to do with it."

"I know," she said. "I don't think he did. But that picture meant something to Chad. Otherwise why would he have kept it?"

"I don't know. I wish to hell he had mentioned something about it, but we haven't found any reference yet in his notes."

"And that would mean either he only got that photograph just before he died, or he didn't think anything of it."

"It was a recent photo for Chad to investigate," Talon

said, his voice low. "It's dated five days before your brother's death."

She stared at him in horror. "We need to talk to my ex-husband."

"We do," he said. "That is, if you can get him to talk to you."

She sat up, reached across him, picked up a tissue off her night table, and wiped her eyes. "For the last year, all I've done is cry. And since you've arrived, it seems like the little bit of control I had slowly gained, I've lost again."

"I'm sorry we didn't come with good news or easy news. But you are handling it just fine."

"Is it wrong to say I don't give a damn about any of it? I just want Chad back." She sniffled and blew her nose.

He understood how she felt. He just lay here, watching as she tried to compose herself. She was still so damn beautiful. She and Chad had been the same in many ways, yet each with their own unique characteristics. He'd been all laughter and light, and she'd been a different kind of light, full of fiery temper and passion. He gently stroked her back and shoulders.

"I'm sorry I walked away." His words startled him.

She turned and stared at him, her gaze wide. "Why did you?"

"I was hurt, tired, fed up with the fighting," he admitted. "I needed to be in the navy. It was a part of me, and I couldn't get you to understand."

She nodded. "I'm not sure I could have back then. I was very insecure. All I was thinking about was myself. I wasn't thinking about you."

He smiled. "I was thinking about myself too. I really wanted to leave, as in *I wanted to save the world.*" His laugh was short and bitter. "And I did some of that. A lot of the work I did was for the good of many people." He felt his body and heart tug at the reminder. "So it's a little hard that, when I needed saving, the assistance wasn't quite what I'd hope for."

She stared at him. "You had multiple surgeries, lots of people looking after you. You've got prosthetics and a whole new future ahead of you. What is it they didn't help you with?"

"It's not even so much that. It's a sense of betrayal because of my team's accident. Our vehicle was deliberately sent on a different road planted with an antitank land mine. The original route we were supposed to take that morning was diverted to the new one. We have intel with a voice sending us on the new route."

She stared at him, not comprehending for a moment. "So you're saying your accident wasn't an accident?"

"That's exactly what I'm saying. But we only recently found out and have gathered what we know in the last couple weeks. So I'm adjusting to a lot of different information too. I don't quite understand what I'm supposed to do with it. In many ways it feels like I'm in quicksand, and all I want is a solid foundation."

She reached out a hand and grasped his. "Even if it was deliberate, you have beat that. You survived."

"But our friend Mouse didn't," he said, sitting up.

"Hence, why this all surrounds him. Somebody wanted him to come home, and he didn't. They're making you pay," she said quietly. She stroked his cheek. "They don't care that you've been through a horrible time yourself. They don't care that there was nothing you could do to save Mouse. All they care about is that their life is now bereft."

"How do you know there was nothing I could do to save Mouse?" he asked.

She smiled. "Because you're a guardian angel. That's who you are. You always have been on the inside. I recognized it. I just didn't want you to go off and save other people. I wanted you to stay here and be with me."

"You were always in my heart though." He hopped to his feet, knowing this would be a difficult conversation if he didn't switch it around. "Why don't you contact your husband and say you found something in the safe you want to talk to him about."

"*Ex*-husband. Keep that in mind, okay?"

"Will do."

"Good," she stood, walked to the bathroom, and washed her face. When she was done, she pulled out her cell phone from her pocket and dialed her ex-husband. "Jerry, it's Clary. I found something in Chad's safe. I wonder if I could meet you somewhere and show it to you, see if you know what it is?"

"What time?"

She checked the time on her cell phone. "I'll meet you at the coffee shop in an hour." She pocketed her cell phone and turned to Talon. "Is that close enough?"

"That's perfect. Let's see if there's anything else of interest in the office. While we're at the coffee shop, we can ask him more questions."

She chuckled. "He won't answer anything. He doesn't like confrontations."

"No? Is he the kind to go behind your back?"

"If it gets the job done, he will, without thinking about it. All he wants is to get his plans accomplished in a nice, neat, orderly fashion. He often cuts out the middleman if it causes him trouble."

Talon had to think about that as they went downstairs. Was it possible this guy, her ex, had decided to cut her out or to cut Chad out, in order to make his job easier? Or more profitable? Was he really trying to get half of the house value? Talon considered what house prices were like in San Diego now and realized Clary was probably sitting on a million-dollar property. And then he thought about all the people he knew and how many would kill for five bucks and just what people would do for half a million dollars. If Jerry had been still married to her when she got the house, and then something happened to Clary … Well then, the ex-husband would inherit it all.

Unfortunately it happened way too often. Nothing was more dangerous than an unhappy spouse. Particularly one who had plans for money that wasn't his.

But the divorce had been finalized weeks earlier, so why would he bother going after Clary now?

CHAPTER 9

SHE WALKED INTO the coffee shop. It was one of the old haunts she and Jerry had frequented over the years. She took her favorite place in a booth at the far side by the window as both Laszlo and Talon went up and ordered coffee. She really didn't need more caffeine. She swore her belly was sloshing around with the stuff now. But, at the same time, it was part of their cover.

She sat quietly, staring out the window. She had her purse in her lap and the envelope inside. They hadn't found anything else in the office, except that the biker apparently was the registered owner of a blue Audi. And that was the news that had set her rocking back on her heels. It seemed like the partial plate they'd seen on the photos she'd had taken had given them the same name she already knew. John MacArthur. And they now had an address for this MacArthur guy. That he'd actually asked to rent the house just a month ago had her nerves jangling badly. When a shadow moved across her face, she looked up to see Jerry smiling down on her.

"Hello, Clary."

She smiled. "Hi, Jerry. Thanks for coming."

He slid into the booth across from her. "All this cloak-and-dagger stuff. You could have just told me what was going on over the phone."

"Sorry, I figured this was easier," she admitted. "I know you and Chad weren't always close. That's why, when I saw this photo in the safe, I wondered what the heck was going on with it."

He studied her for a moment, then looked at the brown envelope she now held in her hand "A photo that size?"

She nodded. "Yeah, I guess it's been blown up." She held up the envelope and slowly withdrew the picture. She had her cell phone beside her. She made as if there was a message coming in and set it up for video, placing it on her purse, propped up against the top. She then held out the picture for him, so she was taping his reaction.

He took one look, and his eyebrows popped up. "Wow. When did he get that?"

"I didn't say he got it," she corrected. "I just said it was in Chad's safe."

"I didn't even know there was a safe in that house," he said with a chuckle.

Was it her imagination, or was that chuckle slightly forced?

He took the picture, studied it close, then laid it on the table, and shrugged. "When did he take it?"

"I didn't say he took it himself either." She leaned back ever-so-slightly and frowned. "It's dated five days before he died."

Immediately a sober understanding whispered across his face.

She hated that about him. He always could make it sound like he understood what she was thinking; then he would do his best to show her how wrong she was.

"Of course anything close to his death makes you suspicious. You know you really shouldn't be working for criminal lawyers. It hasn't been a good thing for you. I'm sure seeing this makes you think all kinds of horrible things. But honestly it was innocent."

"Good," she said lightly. "Who is that guy?"

"John MacArthur," he said with a frown. "I think that's the name anyway."

"What are you talking about?"

He made a face and said, "I think he was asking to rent your parents' house."

Her heart sank. Because that's exactly what MacArthur had asked her too. "What did you tell him?"

"I told him it wasn't for rent."

"And then what did he say?"

"He asked about your brother's house, but I told him that Chad was living in it. The guy just kind of chuckled and said he had heard the man was dead. And then he rode away. See? It was perfectly innocent."

She stared at him. "He said what?"

Jerry repeated what he said. "Like I said, it was completely innocent."

She stared at him. "Or he was the man who killed Chad."

Jerry shook his head. "No, no, no. Don't even go down that road. Your brother was in a terrible accident, remember?"

"Actually he wasn't," a hard voice said beside him.

She looked up to find Talon and Laszlo standing with their coffees.

Talon added in a chilly voice, "Chad was murdered."

TALON STUDIED THE man across the table from Clary. So, this was her ex-husband. Talon couldn't say he was impressed. Although he wouldn't be the first to admit he might be biased. He set a coffee cup gently in front of her. "Just as you ordered." He sat beside her in the booth. Laszlo, by contrast, stood and leaned against the booth. He could have grabbed another chair and pulled it up to their table, but Talon knew Laszlo was blocking Jerry, in case he chose not to stick around.

Jerry frowned at Talon in disbelief. "What are you talking about?"

"Chad was murdered," Talon said in response. "It's pretty simple to understand."

"No, you're not going to sign up for her neurosis," he protested. "Of course there was no murder. It was a hit-and-run accident."

Talon slowly shook his head. He watched as Clary wrapped her fingers around the coffee almost defensively. He was trying to get some signal from Jerry. But, outside of disbelief and potentially a feeling that Clary had been overreacting initially, Jerry didn't appear to have any subterfuge.

"We already have proof. As a matter of fact, we actually know who did it."

"We?" Jerry asked suspiciously. "Who are you?"

Clary opened her mouth to answer, but Talon beat her to it. "A friend of the family. I'm Talon." He tilted his head toward Jerry and said, "Nice to meet you."

Talon watched as a blend of emotions stirred on Jerry's face. Talon didn't quite understand what was going on, until Jerry leaned back but then didn't stop, as if he couldn't get quite far enough away. "Oh."

Interesting response. "Oh?" Talon asked.

"So you're him," he snapped, his gaze going from Talon to Clary and back. "The reason my wife was never fully into our marriage."

Talon's shock was immediate. At the same time, as much as he hated to think it, he was also delighted. "I'm sorry. I don't understand."

But Jerry wasn't having any of it. "Maybe not. But whatever it was that was between the two of you, she never quite got over. Even when she married me, I knew it wasn't because she wanted to be with me. It was because she didn't want to be alone."

"That's not fair," Clary snapped, stepping into the conversation for the first time.

"No, it wasn't fair. Not to me. You said all the right things, did all the right things. But you didn't do them with heart. I couldn't quite figure it out. I thought you were just less emotional, more of a distant person. I thought it would improve with time. Instead, you got more distant, more disinterested in our future." As if he realized he'd never had a chance, or as if he was past caring, he said, "Now I see why." He waved at Talon. "It was always him. Even now, it's all about him."

Talon turned to look at Clary and didn't see anything except for the pink wash of color on her cheeks. But whether that was embarrassment or temper, he couldn't tell. Because her eyes were glittering angrily at her ex.

"That's not true."

His shoulders were already slumping farther. "Hell yes, it's true. But then you weren't ever honest with me. So why the hell would you be honest with yourself at this point?" He slid his way to the end of the table. "I didn't have anything to do with Chad's death. No, he didn't say that, but, just in case you're thinking it, it had nothing to do with me."

At that moment Laszlo stepped forward, blocking his escape. "Why would you think we came here to ask that?" His tone was curious, yet with a thread of steel in it.

Talon was too busy studying Jerry's facial expression to worry about Laszlo.

Jerry settled back in the booth and glared. "She hasn't talked to me, unless it was about the divorce proceedings, in a year. Now all of a sudden, she finds out her brother was murdered, and she brings a photograph of me and some guy, who I presume you think murdered him, and now I'm sitting here with you two bodyguard-type dudes." He shook his head. "But I don't intimidate easily. And there are cops having coffee just a few tables away."

"Good," Talon said. "Maybe we should invite them over."

Jerry snorted. "You got nothing on me."

"Interesting phrase again," Laszlo said. "We already know who murdered Chad, and it wasn't the guy in the photograph."

Jerry shook his head like a bull in a china shop—a slow, angry motion.

Talon could almost see his muscles bunching for a getaway.

"Then what the hell am I doing here?"

"I wanted to know what your meeting with this MacArthur guy was all about," Clary cried out in a low voice. "But, as usual, you go off your rocker and won't let me explain."

He glared at her. "As usual?" He tapped the table hard with his index finger. "Only one of us went off the rails on a regular basis. And it sure as hell wasn't me. I tried to deal with your temper. And sure, eventually it calmed down. But all that replaced it was disinterest, as if you didn't give a shit about anything anymore. You were going through the days but not with any feeling. You got up because you had to. You went to bed at the end of the day tired, but more because of disinterested boredom. Maybe that's what this is all about. It gives you something exciting in your life. How pathetic that you would actually find your brother's *murder* something to get back into life for."

"That's not fair." There was deep hurt in her voice. "My brother was everything to me."

"Isn't that the truth?" he said. Then he took a deep breath, reached up, and pinched the bridge of his nose. "Look, our marriage is long over. We didn't have anything in common then, and we sure as hell don't have anything in common now. I had no reason to hurt Chad, and I told you this guy wanted to rent your parents' house."

"Where did you meet him?"

He looked down at the photo. "You can see the garage right there."

"Is that the only time you saw him?"

There was a very slight hesitation before he nodded. But Talon had seen it. He knew Laszlo had as well.

"Where else did you see him?" Laszlo asked.

Jerry flipped his gaze to Laszlo. "You don't listen well, do you?" His tone was conversational, but he was trying to cover his tracks, and it was too late.

"Say what you want," Talon stated. "But I will call the cops over if you don't tell us the truth. We both caught the change in your face. We know you're lying now. Chad was my best friend, and I will do everything I can to see him get justice."

At that Jerry laughed. “Do you hear yourself? You already tried to tell me that you had caught the murderer. But now you’re telling me that I lied. You don’t know what the hell you’re talking about.”

“Actually we do. Because there’s more to Chad’s death than just his death. And we want to know the rest of it.”

He shrugged. “I don’t intend to tell you jack shit.”

Just then Clary started to dial her phone.

“Who are you calling?”

“The detective handling Chad’s murder.” Her tone was hard, angry. “Maybe you’ll tell the authorities the truth when they haul you in for questioning. I’ll be sure to take pictures of you going into the police station and post it on social media. See how your bosses like that.”

“You think I’ll fall for intimidation?” He shook his head. “Like hell.” He leaned forward. “I couldn’t wait to make that divorce final. I couldn’t wait to get you the hell out of my life.”

She stared at him.

Talon reached across the table, his hand covering hers as she was about to hit Send. “There’s an awful lot of hate there for somebody who says he knows nothing.”

Jerry shrugged irritably. “Too many issues were involved in our relationship, but one thing has nothing to do with the other.”

“That may be, but you’re only acting this way because we want to know where else you met this man. And that’s suspicious enough for me to contact the detective on Chad’s case,” she said. She lifted her gaze. “I know you don’t believe me, but I did come to the same conclusion that I cheated you out of a two-way marriage. No, I didn’t cheat *on* you, but I cheated you from a full relationship. What I thought was love was maybe complacency. What I thought was happy-ever-after was just comfortable. And for that, I'm sorry." Her tone was sad. "I can see how you might feel cheated. But whatever you've done, I didn't deserve it. You could have walked away at any time. You didn't have to wait so long. I get that you're angry. I get that you're upset. I get that you think it was not fair. But I am not that bad of a person that you have to hurt me."

Her words surprised Talon. Her tone of voice, the respect she accorded her ex, was something he hadn't expected. He admired her for it. He didn't think it would be enough to shake loose whatever was going on with Jerry, but at least maybe it would help her clear her conscience.

Jerry stared at her in surprise and then almost in embarrassment as he nodded. "I'm glad you've at least come to that realization. Too bad we both wasted so many years."

She nodded. "You're right. It wasn't just you wasting your life. It was also me."

He shrugged as if he didn't care about what she did with her life.

Talon knew enough about relationships to know it was never just about one person. And sure, she might not have showed up 100 percent for the relationship, but at least she showed up. If he hadn't been happy with what she'd been able to give, then it was on him for having stayed. He glanced from one to the other. "Now tell us where you saw this guy."

Jerry groaned and slumped in his chair. "It's not that big a deal."

"Then tell us," Laszlo said. "If you didn't have anything to do with Chad's death, then at least give Clary the peace of mind of knowing her ex-husband didn't kill her brother in order to get a bigger piece of the pie when you divorced her."

Jerry's gaze widened. "Oh, my God. Is that what you think I did?" He was almost yelling by the time he finished his question. He stared at her, the color bleaching from his cheeks. "Did you know me at all?"

"I did," she said firmly. "Until you became so angry at the end."

"So frustrated. So fed up. So lost. Because, no matter what I did, it didn't seem to make any difference. You didn't care. Your whole world was this pathetic 'okay' zone. I couldn't get you angry. I couldn't get you passionate. I couldn't get anything out of you. You went through your days by rote but showed no expression, no change, no joy, no sadness, no anger." He shook his head. "But to actually think I'd murder Chad? I knew him too, you know? He was my friend."

"You never liked him," she said tiredly. "And he never liked you. You two were amiable at best, and you were pleasant because I was in the middle. But that's the only relationship you had."

His jaw dropped. "Wow. You really have come to some interesting personal growth, haven't you? At least you understand that much. But I respected him. I didn't have to like the man. No, he wasn't my best friend, but I respected that he was your brother. I respected how he went to work every day, came home, paid his bills, and was a law-abiding citizen. I grieved when we lost him. You don't know about that because, of course, you didn't care. You were so caught up in your own world … You felt so alone, but you wouldn't reach out to me for comfort. But I grieved too."

Talon studied him and heard the truth and sincerity and the sadness in his voice. He believed him. "So then tell us. If you had nothing to do with Chad's death, and you weren't expecting half of the house she'd just inherited, why did you meet with this man?"

"He told me that he had photos of Clary. Photos that she'd been unfaithful."

And his words fell on the heavy silence like a bomb going off. Talon turned to look at Clary and asked, "Is it true?"

She switched her gaze to Talon.

He could see her hurtful expression. And the pain in her features. Not from her ex-husband's accusation but from Talon questioning her honor and ethics.

But she turned toward her ex and nearly threw the words at him. "No, it's not true. The one thing I was, even if I was much less than you had hoped for, was faithful."

CHAPTER 10

SHE DIDN'T THINK she'd ever recover from these personal assaults. It felt like the last couple years had been nothing but blow after blow after blow. But coming to meet Jerry for coffee, that was the pinnacle of pain. To think how he had felt about their relationship, their marriage, after all these years. And to know he'd been right was something she would never forgive herself for. She should never have married him. She should have broken it off a long time ago—but then he should have too.

But to think this asshole in the photo was trying to stir the pot and to imply she'd been unfaithful in any way and that Jerry would actually meet him, believing such a thing, was devastating.

But even all of that was nothing to the pain she felt when Talon had glanced over at her and had asked her about the truth. She was frozen. And angry. And she wanted nothing to do with anyone right now. And yet she was caught, pinned inside the booth by Talon who faced Jerry, with Laszlo a curious onlooker. And she knew there was nothing she could say to convince these men who had already questioned her morals.

She turned to stare out the window, refusing to say anything else. She didn't know what the conversation was about anymore. She wasn't listening. She just shut down.

When her phone rang, she stared at it restlessly. She didn't even know the number. She finally hit Talk. "Hello?"

"Having fun?" said a lighthearted voice on the other end.

"It depends what you call fun." She frowned as she tried to recognize her caller. "Who is this?"

"Well, maybe you'd like to see the photos your ex-husband's telling you about now."

She stiffened, her gaze going to Jerry. "How do you know I'm visiting with my ex-husband right now?" She could feel Talon and Laszlo snapping to attention.

"I have my ways," the caller mocked.

She turned the phone on Speaker so everyone could hear the conversation. Jerry's jaw dropped. He went to open his mouth, but Laszlo slapped a hand over it.

"What do you want?" She just wanted this all over with—all of it. "You want me dead? Then shoot me. Take me out of the equation. I don't give a shit."

"Wow. You know that's no fun. Kicking a dog who'll fight back, well, that's one thing, but kicking a dog already down, who doesn't do anything but whimper and lie there waiting for the next blow? That almost makes you an abused wife."

She snorted. "No, he'd have to care to do that." She stared into Jerry's angry eyes. "He's too busy blaming me to look at his own failings. Whatever. You don't have any photos because they don't exist. If you created anything, they're just altered by Photoshop and can be disproven. Who gives a crap?"

The man on the other end chuckled. "Wow. You really are despondent, aren't you? Suicidal yet?"

"No. Is that what you're hoping for?" she asked with a note of interest in her voice. "Can't say in all the years I was married to a man who didn't give a shit about me that I became suicidal. I highly doubt I would be now. Chad's been gone for a year. Did you have something to do with his death?"

"No, but an associate did. Money will buy you anything."

She froze. "You're the one who paid for his murder?" She stared down at the phone, anger vibrating throughout her entire system. "Why?"

"Well, to hurt Talon of course. And, of course, Talon is sitting right beside you."

But Laszlo was no longer around. He'd disappeared from sight. Talon stayed right beside her, although he nudged her away from the window.

"Why do you hate Talon so much?" she asked, wishing she knew who she was talking to.

"Maybe it's not about hate. Maybe it's about making him suffer."

"Maximum pain?"

He chuckled. "That's a very good phrase. I like that. I'll have to use it."

"Why, because Mouse died? So you go around and kill anybody close to him? What kind of a man are you?"

"A vindictive one," he snapped. "And you don't know jack shit." And he hung up.

She held her hands out to see them shaking. She immediately clasped them together and shoved them into her lap. She stared at Jerry who gazed at her in horror.

"What the hell was that?"

She shook her head. "Don't worry about it. Go back to your nice little life, you and your house of lies you've built."

He stared at her. "You really think I didn't love you?"

"No, you didn't love me," she said sadly. "You loved the thought of having a wife and how we would have that perfect family. But you chose me for the exact same reasons I chose you. Because it was comfortable. Because you didn't want to get hurt. Because your first wife died from cancer and it tore you apart. I was the replacement. But I was a healthy replacement, an easy replacement, one who didn't ask much of you, one you didn't have to worry about feeling too strongly for. And, when we got divorced, it was easy to blame me. But you never once looked at your part in it. Marriage is a two-way street. And, yes, I didn't show up fully, but neither did you. Now take a hike. I'll be happy to not have to see you again."

She watched as he almost bolted from the restaurant. She had no idea if a bullet would end up in his forehead, and she hated to admit it, but, at that moment, she didn't care. And that wasn't good either. The caller was right about one thing: she was pretty despondent. Some things about her life were difficult, and, if she could find a way out of this nightmare, she'd take it in a heartbeat. If there was a bullet out there with her name on it, she wasn't terribly upset about that either.

She stared out the window and didn't have anything more to say.

Talon wrapped an arm around her shoulders and tucked her up close. "Obviously it's been a very tough day."

She snorted. "You think?"

"We can't leave just yet. Laszlo's checking outside."

She shrugged. "Whatever." She felt more than saw his sharp gaze.

"What happened to the fire and spice in the girl who I left behind?"

"Well, when you hate yourself enough, it doesn't really matter what happens to you because nobody else can hurt you more than you've already hurt yourself."

"What do you hate yourself for?" he asked with outrage. "You're incredible. You've done so well. You're bright and intelligent, and you're beautiful."

She lifted deadened eyes and turned to him. "I chased you away. That's what I hate myself for."

TALON FELT LIKE a knife had seared through his heart. But he could see the truth laid bare in her eyes. The pain that she'd never quite dealt with. The well of hurts she'd stuffed deep inside. And the self-loathing she'd lived with all these years.

He muttered, "Jesus," and tugged her tighter into his arms. He sat there, just holding her against his chest, half on his lap, half off. They were in a restaurant, a public place, definitely not ideal. He knew she wouldn't totally break down. But he wished she'd do something. Today had hurt her, slicing off little layers until she'd been exposed for who and what she really was. He suspected she'd always known but had done her best to hide it because how did one live with all that for others to see?

She straightened after a moment and called the waitress over. "May I get more coffee please?"

The waitress came and filled her cup. Clary pushed her phone toward him. "Can you trace that?"

"Chances are it'll be a burner phone." He accepted her change of topic to put distance between them, at least for now. He pulled out his own phone and sent a text. He did something to her phone, but she had no idea what. And she didn't really care.

Laszlo slipped onto the bench across from them. "No sign of him."

"But he was here, right?" Clary asked.

"Unless it was a wild guess. Did you tell Jerry that Talon and I would be with you?"

She shook her head. "No, I just arranged to meet him here at the restaurant."

"So then we have to assume somebody saw us arrive. Likely followed us here."

She nodded. "He's always one step ahead, isn't he?"

"Often that's the way it is." Laszlo gave her a slight smile. "But they don't stay that way. They do make mistakes eventually."

"He did this time too," she said.

"Why is that?"

"Because he didn't deny what I said about Mouse. And you guys need to tear apart Mouse's life one stone at a time until you find out who this person is."

Both men nodded.

"Agreed." Laszlo looked at her cup. "You ordered another coffee?"

She stared down at it.

Talon studied her face. "If you don't want it, we can leave."

She nodded. "I just want to go home."

Worried about her, but hoping to get back to his laptop where he could continue with what he needed to do, Talon nodded. "Come on. Let's go."

CHAPTER 11

SHE WAS BACK home in her bedroom, lying on her bed, before she even became aware of having moved from the coffeehouse. She'd been so stunned, so in shock, and just numb to everything that, when Talon had moved her out of the restaurant, into the vehicle, and back home again, she'd gone along without protest, without thinking. It said much about her level of trust in Talon. Knowing he'd care for her and look after her.

Some pretty hard truths had been spoken at the table with her ex-husband.

How sad to think that those were words that should have been spoken before the marriage, at least sometime during the marriage. Instead, they'd each stored them up until they'd come out, well past the divorce. When it was too late to change anything. She had a lot to think about.

No doubt that Talon's presence had been a catalyst for much of this. She'd never thought to see him again. And she'd never thought to lose her brother. But both of those events had occurred, and she was still adjusting to each. Chad had been gone a year. But to think Talon might come back into her life was a joy she didn't dare count on. She was willing to work to make it happen. She just didn't know how to begin to repair the damage done to her relationship with him.

According to her ex-husband, she'd never gotten over Talon. According to herself, she'd always loved him. How sad was that?

She lay on her bed, staring at the wall in front of her. She might even have had a short nap. She felt better. She didn't know what time it was and didn't want to roll over to look. When the bed beside her moved, she froze.

"It's all right. I've just been lying here beside you."

Slowly she rolled to her back. And, sure enough, there was Talon, smiling at her. "Why?" Even that didn't sound like her. Her voice was froggy, hoarse.

"Because I'm worried about you," he admitted. "You've always been very special to me. You had some pretty major shocks and a lot of trauma this last year."

She let her eyes drift closed as she rolled back over again. "Nothing like you had."

"It's not a contest. My shocks were physical. Yours were emotional."

She gave a harsh sound and pushed herself up to a sitting position. She pulled the blanket he'd thrown across her up to her chest and stared at him. "I highly doubt there weren't any emotional issues for you to deal with when you lost your leg and your arm."

"No, and the loss of the leg was easier than the loss of my arm," he admitted. "I knew I could get around without the leg. I've known many men who have lost a foot or a leg. The hand seemed to be a lot more difficult. But this prosthetic is so much more advanced that I'm quite happy to live with it. It's also my left arm and hand, but, as I'm right-handed, that works."

She reached out a hand, realizing he was no longer wearing a long-sleeve shirt. She stared at his prosthetic arm for a long moment. "You should leave it like that."

"Like what?"

"Uncovered. It's pretty cool looking." She shuffled over for a better look. "It's also a sign you're a little more relaxed around me that you're not trying to hide it."

He didn't say anything for a long moment. And then out of the blue, he asked, "Was Jerry correct?"

Startled, she studied his face to figure out what he was asking. There was heat in his gaze that found a responding heat in her heart. "You mean, the part about never getting over you? The part where I said I hated myself for what I did?" She nodded. "Yes. Already said so. I felt like I'd ruined something very special. Something I would never get again. And I think I just shut down a part of me. Jerry was second-best. He was right about that, but then I was second-best for him too. It's always easier to judge others than it is to look at ourselves."

"Did you ever love him?"

She brushed her hair off her forehead, hating this conversation. "I thought I did." She was tired and frustrated. "But obviously I didn't."

"Did you ever love me?"

Her eyes flew wide open. "Yes. I did."

He seemed to search deep inside her through her eyes, as if searching for the truth. He sagged back as if believing her.

And that just made her angrier. "How could you doubt that?" she cried out sadly. "The same as how could you ask me if it was true about me having an affair?"

"Because people lie all the time. And people also change."

She shook her head and swung her legs off the bed, getting up, going into the bathroom. After using the facility, she stared in the mirror for a long moment. She didn't know what had happened, but she felt like she was in a completely different zone. Not comfortable with everything so raw. Not happy but not sad, more drained. As if everything had been pulled out of her. Exposed for everyone to see.

Knowing she still had to go out and face him, she opened the door and stepped into her room. He was on his laptop working, propped up against her bed. "Why are you here?"

He raised his eyes. "Originally or right now?"

"Right now."

"Because I care. And I hate to see you so shattered."

She thought about his description and realized it was true. "My broken marriage, Chad's death, the divorce … It started a … a weird cycle. And this last year, I thought I was recovering. But I wasn't. I was just holding on. Trying to get through every day. And then today …" She opened her arms as if to say she didn't understand what it was. "It was painful."

"Of course it was," he said gently. "It would have been nice if that conversation had happened before you'd gotten married. But the fact that it didn't, and it came out now, is at least something. Maybe you can both walk away from what you had to find something better."

"I don't know. I appear to be a failure at relationships."

"Why? Because you've got one marriage behind you? A lot of people have multiple divorces behind them."

"That's not reassuring. I don't want to be like that."

"Did you have other relationships?"

She knew what he was asking. "I did. But they weren't as intense as ours and certainly not as long as the one I had with Jerry."

"Had you given up by the time you met Jerry?"

"I think he was just safe. Good enough. And, in that, he was right. I definitely cheated him."

"And you've acknowledged it. You've apologized. You've stepped up, and now it's time to put it away and move on." He spoke the words firmly.

That forced a laugh out of her. "Is it that easy?"

"It doesn't have to be any harder."

She looked at the laptop. "Did you find any more answers? Do we believe him, what he said about this guy with the pictures?"

"I contacted Jerry since we left and got a little more information about it. He sounded strange, like he's going through a similar self-identity crisis, like you are. He had showed up at the meeting with MacArthur, but the guy didn't have any photos. Just an empty envelope. He was just laughing at him. Telling him that he should trust his wife."

"So why didn't he tell us that?"

"Because he felt foolish. He should have trusted you. But he jumped at a chance to see something that would give him a reason to walk away."

She nodded and walked to the bedroom window. "Isn't that the truth? So we really need to focus on who this guy is, find him, see why he's interfering in my life."

"That sums it up," Talon said cheerfully. "The good news is, chances are this is the guy we want and not anybody else. I can't imagine you have two men stalking you."

"I shouldn't have even one." There was a knock on her bedroom door. "Come in."

Laszlo pushed open the door and looked at the two of them. "Just got word from Erick. He's confirmed the hit man's connection to two other deaths within our families.

An associate did the actual hits."

"Really?" Talon jumped to his feet, his laptop barely making it to the bed as he stood. "Does he have any names for us to go on?"

"He's still digging. I sent him all the photographs we had on Clary's stalker, the photo of MacArthur and Jerry, and the information from Clary's caller today. Erick said he should have an identity for us soon as to the second hit man on two of our family members."

"What good will that do?" she asked. "You think it is our blue Audi guy, right? We already have an identity. John MacArthur."

The two men looked at her and shook their heads. "It's an alias."

"Of course it is," she said sarcastically. "You realize I don't live in that world?" It was all a bit convoluted for her. But, as long as they understood what the hell they were talking about, she'd leave it to them to handle. She walked with them downstairs. "Even if we do get his real name, and we get an address, then what will you do? Talk to him?"

"Hell yes. In fact, we already have one address for him." He turned to Laszlo. "Let's see if Erick confirms that one as a valid address before we speak with him."

She frowned. "And, if you scare him to death, will that stop him?"

"It's hard to say. It seems like we're leaving a body count wherever we go. The ultimate boss man is killing off his minions. If this guy doesn't quite survive our encounter, I've got no problem with that." Laszlo's voice came out in a cool tone. "A lot of assholes are in this world. We could do without a couple of them."

She turned to stare at him to see if he was joking, but

nothing in his chiseled jawline said he was. That reminded her once again how many dead bodies these hit men were responsible for. "Do you really think it's related to Chad's murder? They were probably stalking me to kill me."

"That's what we think," Laszlo said cheerfully. "Then they chose Chad."

"Great. Am I supposed to feel good about that?" Her voice held the bitterness she felt. "You know I'd rather be dead than him, don't you?"

"Life didn't give you a choice," Talon reminded her. "And we can't change anything now."

She walked into the kitchen. "We were at a coffee shop, and we didn't eat."

"Breakfast was hours ago," Laszlo said. "If you're offering more food, I won't say no."

She turned to look at him, caught sight of the clock behind him, and frowned. "Did I sleep for a couple hours?"

"About two," Talon said. "Are you feeling better?"

She stopped to think about it, then nodded. "Actually I am."

The trouble was, she wasn't terribly hungry. She knew she needed to eat just to keep the stomach acid at bay. But the rest of it, the words exchanged today, the killer's phone call to her, well, made her feel old and incredibly tired. She stared blindly into the fridge.

Talon got up and nudged her toward the table. "You sit down. I'll find something for lunch."

"It's almost dinnertime," she said. "It's four."

"So maybe we'll have an early dinner." He glanced at the fridge. "Do you have any meat or shall we order in something?"

She shrugged. "I don't care what you order in, but, if it's

pizza, make sure it doesn't have any pineapple on it."

"What?" Laszlo piped up. "Pineapple is the best."

She snorted. "Only loony tunes put pineapple on their pizza. Fruit does not go anywhere near bread and meat."

He stared at her in fascination. "But you're okay with anchovies?"

She wrinkled up her nose. "Not my favorite but, sure, that's fish."

"Wow, so you're an all-meat type of person." Laszlo nodded. "I can get behind that." He glanced over at Talon. "Why don't we get an order from Johnny's?"

Talon looked at him, a big smile breaking across his face. "Haven't had that in a long time."

"Best pizza in town," Laszlo said.

"I've never even heard of it," Clary protested. "How good could it possibly be?"

Talon smiled. "You have no idea."

TALON HAD RESUMED researching at Laszlo's side while Clary grabbed a book and curled up in the corner of the living room couch. Since she had stayed in there, they had moved their work to the living room as well.

Talon kept an eye on her, making sure she was okay, that the pages were turning and that she seemed engaged in the story. What he didn't want was for her to get maudlin about all that had come up today. It would take her a while to adjust to the new situation in her life that she found herself in. He returned his gaze to his laptop. That's when the doorbell rang, and the pizza delivery arrived, just over an hour after ordering them.

Laszlo got up and paid for the pizzas as Talon nudged Clary into the kitchen. Quietly she followed his prompting and preceded him into the room. He was more than a little worried about the quiet state she was in. Not quite on automation but not far off. He smiled when he saw the three extra large pizzas.

She stared. "You're not expecting me to eat a whole one, are you?"

"Nope. But this way I don't need more food for the rest of the day," Laszlo said with a grin. He efficiently flipped the tops over and under so all three boxes could sit on the table.

One extra large pizza had pineapple completely covering the top. Talon chuckled. "Well, we know which one yours is."

"Absolutely." Laszlo gave him a fat smile as he pulled the ham and pineapple pizza toward himself.

Talon happened to catch Clary's fascinated gaze and her mock shudder as Laszlo bit into a slice. She picked up a slice laden with all different kinds of meat. "What's on the third one?" Talon asked.

"I told him to surprise me but no fruit."

"Good enough for me." So Talon started with that one.

The conversation stayed light and easy. After Clary finished her first piece, Talon nudged the second box toward her. "Eat more," he urged.

Obediently she picked up a second piece and ate it. He exchanged a glance with Laszlo. Both could see she was in a different place that they didn't recognize. But it wasn't healthy—at least not for too long.

Talon and Laszlo kept a running dialogue going, hoping to distract her or to engage her, but she seemed off in her own world.

The next time he glanced at the clock it was almost six o'clock. The whole evening yawned ahead of them. What she needed was sleep. But he didn't know how to get her there and how to ensure she got a decent night. Even with her earlier two-hour nap, she needed a solid eight more tonight. Something physical would help. But she didn't have a pool. "Do you want to go for an after-dinner walk?" he asked her, yet he still was eating his pizza.

She glanced at him in surprise. But she didn't say no immediately. She thought about it and then shrugged. "We could."

There it was again, that same *I don't care what we do* kind of thing. He wondered if that was how she'd been throughout her marriage. That would have driven him insane. He had another piece of pizza as he thought about it. They were still in the city, but they could walk in certain places with relative safety. There were parks around, or they could just walk several blocks. He decided to do that.

After dinner they left the rest of the pizza in one box and took the empty pizza boxes out to the recycling bin. With her dressed in walking shoes, he left Laszlo behind to hold down the fort.

Tucking her hand into his elbow, Talon walked Clary up the street and around the block. They continued on for a good ten to fifteen minutes in silence. It was still warm outside, the sun high in the sky. In a way he wanted to wait a little bit longer, until it had cooled down, but it was nice enough outside. There was a park up ahead, he remembered. He kept walking in that general direction until they came to it.

He motioned to a bench by the flower gardens. "Do you want to sit for a few minutes?"

"Doesn't matter," she said.

"It does matter," he said forcefully. "Either you're tired and would like to sit, or you'd like to sit here and just enjoy the garden, or we can keep walking."

She shot him a hooded gaze. "Then we can sit for a bit."

He led her to the bench, and they sat down. There was a large rose garden with annuals all around the base. In the evening the heavy aroma from the roses was striking. He sat back and relaxed ever-so-slightly. He really enjoyed his exercising, but sometimes, during his recovery, a walk was all he could have done. Thankfully he was long past that point, but many times his therapist had insisted he just get up and keep walking.

Jim, his trainer, used to say, "It doesn't matter if you want to or not. The minute you start moving, endorphins get released. And it helps you to feel better about what you're doing, and suddenly you want to do more. This isn't a case of *I'll stay in bed and let the world go by*. This is a case of, *if you put one foot in front of the other, soon enough something comes along that helps you to feel better*." It had taken a while, but Talon had finally believed him.

After a few minutes, she continued to just sit here, not saying a thing. He hopped to his feet and said, "Okay, let's go on."

She turned to look at him. "And what if I'm happy here?"

"Too bad. You're still in that same mood. Time to pick it up a bit." He reached down, grabbed her hand gently, and helped her to her feet. "Come on. Let's go."

"What difference will it make?"

He nudged her forward. "Anything that takes you out of the self-pity you're in is a good thing."

"I'm not feeling self-pity," she snapped.

Inside he grinned. Anger was way healthier than that crazy silent, sullen mood of hers. "Good, glad to hear it."

"You don't believe me, do you?"

"I don't have to believe you. *You* have to believe *you*. Because otherwise you'll slide back into that weird mood."

"A lot of hard truths were voiced today. I just need a good night's sleep."

Privately he didn't agree with that simple reassurance. It would take more than one day to deal with those hard truths. But he had faith in her to do just that. They walked quietly. He kept moving her through the blocks and up and down the streets.

Finally she said, "How long do you want to walk?"

"Until you feel better," he said.

"I felt better a while ago," she muttered.

"I know. It was somewhere around the time you snapped at me."

She sighed. "He's right, you know? I never got angry."

"And yet with me, you're always this fiery personality."

"You set me off."

He chuckled. "And you already knew that the marriage was a mistake. But it's brought you to this stage of self-understanding. A lot of people would say, *Nothing is a mistake, and that this is good. Now you can move on.*"

"Move on to what?"

"I don't know." He was trying to keep upbeat. "What would you like to do?"

"Not go back to work tomorrow."

"I thought you liked your job?"

"I haven't for a while."

"Then change it. Sell Chad's house. A ton of money is

tied up in that place. You can do anything you want."

"I'm not sure I'm ready to do that."

"Then don't sell it. Find something you do want to do and make that house decision later."

Privately he was thinking she would be better off to move totally away. He wasn't sure it was terribly healthy to sit in this big old house of Chad's with another empty family house beside her. It would only make her life feel lonely. "Unless you want to hang on to it for sentimental reasons."

She shook her head. "I did. But now that I've been there for a whole year, it's not the same. It just feels like a big old drafty house. But you know? I felt tied to it."

"Possessions can become chains. I didn't own anything for a long time. Not necessarily a good thing but it gave me the freedom to move around as I needed to."

"But you always had a place to come home to. The military gave you housing one way or another."

"Those were always a bed to sleep in," he agreed. "But they weren't home."

"So what did you do when you were on your leaves?"

"I went back to the same bed I always had when I wasn't on leave. It was a place to sleep, but it wasn't home. I spent most of my time with friends or alone. But I didn't have anybody with me."

"Relationships?" she asked with a spark of interest in her voice.

"Yes, many," he admitted. "But none serious."

"Why?"

"Because I already knew what I was doing in the navy wouldn't be what any woman wanted. You had made that very clear. You see? It's not just you hanging onto garbage from way back when."

She was silent for a long moment. "Everything we do really affects those around us, doesn't it?"

"Yes. That's why it's important to show up with integrity in everything you do."

She chuckled. "What are you? Some self-help guru?"

"No, but there's nothing like being on the outside, an observer to all the rest around you, to see how people act and react to each other. Once I realized that what we had earlier wasn't working for us—not some of it anyway—I spent a lot of time studying relationships, trying to figure out what made them work."

"And what made them work?"

He glanced down at her and smiled. "Trust. Honesty. Compassion. Compromise. And most of all, love. With love comes respect." He watched the same troubling look fall on her face again. He winced. "Maybe I shouldn't have said that."

"No. It appears to be the day for it."

"Good. Then tomorrow is a whole new day, and we can forget about it all."

She shook her head. "I don't think we should."

They walked along in companionable silence. Suddenly she stopped, pivoted to look at him. He was standing just under the bough of a large tree. He couldn't take his eyes off her. "What's the matter?" he asked softly.

There was a tremulous look to her lips, her eyes open wide. "Where are we going?"

Even he knew she wasn't talking about location. But he wouldn't be anything less than honest. "Somewhere into the future, I hope." But, of course, he hadn't dared to envision that she would let him back into her life, much less be interested in moving forward together. "Where do you want to go?"

She shook her head impatiently. "No games. You said we need to show up as our authentic selves. Then right now, right here, let's be honest. Show me who you are, and I'll show you who I am."

He started to smile. "Is this where I get to tease you and ask you to show me yours first?"

She glared at him. "I'm serious."

He nodded. "I am too."

She frowned, her gaze searching his.

He sighed and reached out a hand. "You can't really expect me to bare my heart when I have no clue where you're at."

She took a deep breath. "That's true," she admitted. "Okay, so here it goes." She took a step forward until they were almost touching. She tilted her head up to look in his eyes. "I want a second chance."

CHAPTER 12

SHE WATCHED THE look of shock cross his eyes. She resisted the urge to step back, to recoil from what she saw as rejection. But the smile slowly curving his lips upward and the gentleness in his gaze made her stop.

"A second chance, as in you and me?" As if a bit uncertain of the answer, he stated carefully, "I want to be very clear about what we're doing here."

"Exactly. I haven't seen you at all in eight years. Out of the blue you show up, and my life is in complete chaos," she muttered. "But, instead of the chaos I expected to still be in, all of a sudden I'm seeing clearly for the first time in a long time."

"This is sudden," he said cautiously. "We've been through an awful lot ..."

She placed her finger against his lips to stop him. "I've been through enough. So have you. I don't want to be hiding away or broken anymore. I want to step forward and to seize the reins of my life and to do something positive." She could see the understanding, the fear, and the hope as she swept her gaze to his eyes one at a time. "I could always read your emotions in your eyes." Her voice lowered. "But you never would explain. You never said the words to what you were feeling."

He kissed her finger still against his lips. "I want that

second chance too. But I'm the one who walked away."

She shook her head. "I pushed you away. I gave you an ultimatum, never expecting … or maybe I wanted you to choose that. Maybe I was looking to confirm you didn't love me. I was young and stupid," she murmured. "Whatever I was doing back then was foolish. And made no sense. And it doesn't matter now, because it was a long time ago."

"It does matter," he said firmly, "if it affects who and what we are today. Because, if and when we are moving forward together, I don't want to go back to what we had before, not completely."

She smiled tremulously up at him. "Good, because I don't either." She stepped closer, threw her arms around his neck, and kissed him.

And just like it always was, passion swept through her, swept through him, and, where their mouths collided, a heated firestorm erupted. She moaned as her body cried out in joy, recognizing the partner of her heart—the male her body had welcomed each and every time with such joy, with such eagerness. She wanted him as if all those years—questioning his absence and feeling abandoned and hurt and even hating herself—had never happened. The trouble was, she had always wanted him. Now was no different. Somewhere in the dim recesses of her mind, she could hear a tiny mewling sound escaping her lips. And she realized she had one leg wrapped around his hips, already trying to climb his frame.

She broke apart and stepped back, her hand to her cheeks. "Oh, wow." She was in complete shock. "I didn't think that would still happen."

She watched as he struggled to control his passion, his cheeks already red. She dared not sweep down his body, but couldn't resist, and, sure enough, as it had always been before, his erection strained in his jeans, and his hands were gripped in fists so as not to grab her and toss her to the grass. She so eagerly wanted him to do just that.

He closed his eyes for a long moment as she watched him war with his incredible self-control. Yet years ago he had been happy to lose it, under the right circumstances. When they made love, he gave it his all. He didn't hold back, and neither had she. They hadn't known there were games to play in bed. They hadn't known that relationships were dances, sometimes not very nice ones. Back then, when they had been young lovers, they had only been honest with each other, sharing their good and their bad sides, acknowledging who they were inside and how they felt for each other. If only it had been that clear-cut outside of their lovemaking.

She took a deep breath and whispered, "I'm so sorry."

His gaze flew open, and he pinned her in place with that glittering look. "Sorry for what?"

And she was saddened by that need to question what she meant. But she accepted it as where they were, and, until they could trust each other, could know who and where they were, they needed to question everything. Painfully, and yet honestly, as she always had been with him. In bed, without her mind tormenting her outside of the bedroom. "I'm sorry we're not back in my bedroom right now, with the full privacy of a closed door and time to ourselves."

And that smile, when it came, was breathtaking. It swept her off her feet and tossed her down memory lane. He reached out with his hand.

She stared at it for a long moment, then cried out, "Yes," and grasped it.

He turned to look around, as if orienting himself as to

where they were.

And it was a good thing he did because she had no clue. And she didn't want to know. She just wanted the fastest route back to her room.

Suddenly he seemed to understand exactly where they needed to go. He tucked her hand firmly in his, turned her around, and walked forward at an incredibly fast pace.

She was almost running to keep up. And she didn't care. She laughed with joy as he walked faster and faster until they were both jogging along the street, something they used to do all the time.

He never once let go of her hand.

She was surprised when he took several right-hand turns, and suddenly they were on her block. She shook her head. "I was completely lost. I had no clue where we were."

"I did. And I know exactly where we're heading."

Laughing, she tumbled in the front door with him following. She took a moment to turn and lock the door and then raced upstairs to her bedroom. She almost beat him there. But he overtook her right at her bedroom door and caught her in a hot, arousing kiss. She collapsed against him. But he still had the presence of mind to shut the bedroom door, locking it before picking her up, tossing her on the bed.

She opened her arms, her body already wet and willing, waiting, trembling, needing him so much. But he didn't come to her as fast as she had expected. As if he needed her to see him—to see him as he was now—he pulled off his shirt, then quickly stepped out of his jeans, making sure she understood who and what he was as a man.

She smiled when she saw his leg. But the smile fell away when she saw the scars on his body. Tears came to her eyes, and she slid off the bed, her fingers sliding across a huge scar along his abdomen.

She walked around him ever-so-slowly, her fingers stroking, caressing, soothing the multitude of scars and surgical wounds, the damages of the horrific accident that he'd barely survived and then the aftermath he had endured. When she came back around to the front, there was a tiny nick on his chest just off the breastbone, the scar still a good inch wide by maybe a half inch deep.

Overcome with emotions at what he'd been through, she lowered her head and kissed it gently. She wrapped her arms around him and held him close. And still he didn't move to initiate anything, and she realized he needed something so much more from her. She stepped back, and, without dropping her gaze from his, she stripped just as he had. Her body was still the same, although maybe not as fit as it had once been. When she was completely nude before him, she stepped closer and whispered, "Make love with me now."

As if released from a tightly wound elastic band, he snatched her up into his arms, and the two of them fell onto the bed.

She knew there had been foreplay in there somewhere, but she didn't remember anything but heat as it circled every one of her bones, down to her toes, making them curl, before it raced back up, leaving her in agonizing torture as he refused to come to her as she wanted him to. And just when she was beyond frustrated, she reached up, grabbed clumps of his hair, and tugged him down toward her.

Before his lips claimed hers, she whispered, "Now."

And he plunged deep.

She cried out, her body arching beneath him. He froze, and she whispered, "No, it's fine. It's just been so long."

He reached down, held her hips, readjusted himself, and then with a tenderness she had forgotten, he moved his hips gently, slowly. His hands enticed, caressed, stroked, teasingly, as if reacquainting himself with her body that he knew so well.

Just when she didn't think she could handle his slow pace anymore, he whispered, "Sit up."

And she remembered. She sat up, poking her legs outside of his hips, and, with him kneeling, she slowly rode him. But she couldn't do it for long. The pressure, the twisting of emotions, the supreme tension coiled tighter and tighter as she moved faster and faster. His hands on her hips helped her move up and down, as they came together with the same joy and passion they had had so many years ago.

She cried out as a kaleidoscope of feelings exploded within, filling her heart and her mind with joy. She didn't hear him, but she could feel his body erupt, the tension releasing, his arm clenching as he clasped her tight against his body, shuddering in the wake of his own release. Still shuddering, her body still rocking with aftershocks, he slowly laid her down on the bed and shifted to lie beside her.

She murmured, "I'm glad to see that part of your body wasn't injured."

He chuckled, leaned over, kissed her gently, and whispered, "Me too."

She wrapped her arms around him and held him close. "You know that it's not pity I see when I look at you," she said quietly. "Yet I can't help but sympathize for all the pain you went through. Not only the initial pain from the explosion but also the pain of recovery. However, more than that, I respect what you came through to get to this side. I always knew you were a hell of a man. But now … Now I've seen the proof of it." She opened her eyes fully, leaned up, and kissed him with all the tenderness she could muster. "What saddens me, brings tears to my eyes if you ever see them, is that you had to go through it alone. I'd have given everything to sit by your bedside to let you know you were no longer alone."

His gaze darkened, and he rolled over, flattening her beneath him. He didn't say anything; he used his hands and mouth to express just how he felt. She'd never experienced such tenderness, such a sense of being the most precious thing in a man's arms, except with him.

After he'd left for the navy, she'd had several affairs, needing to know that she was still attractive and that maybe somebody would love her. But they hadn't been Talon, and she'd soon stopped seeking to find love in mindless sex. But this night of lovemaking was for them. She hoped for many more. But even as he filled her again, and as her heart was overwhelmed to the point of overflowing, she knew what a gift he'd given her.

"Thank you so much," she whispered.

He stilled in his gentle movements and pulled back slightly to look down at her. He stroked the hair off her face. "Thank me for what?"

She smiled, a little more used to the probing questioning, as she said, "For giving me a second chance."

He dropped a kiss on the tip of her nose, then on her chin and on her cheeks. "Ditto."

And proceeded to love her all over again.

TALON WOKE EARLY in the morning, long before dawn. His

body sore but humming with the sensation that only came with sexual satisfaction. A global well-being. Last night was his first sexual encounter since his accident. It could hardly be called an encounter. It was a homecoming. He'd never even thought she could care after all this time. But to know she'd been waiting inside her heart for him to come back made him wish he'd returned years ago. He tucked her up closer against him, his hand stroking her lower arm. Of course he couldn't feel anything, but, just to know she wasn't intimidated, scared, or disgusted by the man he was now gave him such great hope.

For the longest time he thought he'd never be able to have a relationship again. That he'd never be able to hold a woman in his arms because nobody would ever care to be there. That he'd be so ugly, so broken, so scarred, that it would be a hardship for anyone to love him. Instead, his beautiful generous-of-heart Clary not only hadn't seemed to care about those things, she had barely noticed. When he'd stood before her, bare of everything, so she might see who he was for real, he'd felt like such a shadow of who he'd been with her previously, until she had kissed his scar. Just one of many.

And he realized he'd initially misjudged her. She wasn't pitying him. She was just … loving him. And *that* he'd take anytime. He smiled as he conformed his body to hers, watching the night edge toward morning out her window. He heard her breathing slow down and become more uniform. Knowing they were in good hands with Laszlo downstairs, Talon closed his eyes and drifted off.

The next time he awoke, it was getting lighter outside. Maybe six in the morning. With surprise, he realized he'd had his first decent night's sleep in a long time. He knew he wouldn't have to explain where he was to Laszlo. Clary was still tucked in his arms. He smiled gently remembering all the lazy mornings they'd enjoyed in the past. He didn't know how long he could stay here in San Diego. There wasn't anything back in Santa Fe except for all his friends and Kat. As he lay on the bed, thinking about what it would be like to either move here or to ask her to move with him, she spoke.

"Do you have a house in Santa Fe?"

He nodded. "I do. But it's nothing like this."

"Tell me about it."

"The backyard opens to state land, so there's nobody behind it. It's an extra large lot, the size of four actually, so there are no close neighbors. I don't stare from my windows into the window of another house. You can walk for miles. I have jogging routes, and they start right out my back door. I'm less than three blocks from a large river, and that's another walk I love to take in the afternoon. The house itself isn't spectacular, but it's nice," he continued. "I've been doing a lot of work on it. One of these days I might even finish it." He chuckled. "It was never anything I intended to do, but, after I needed a home, I fell in love with this place and realized it was something I could do for myself, put a piece of my personality into it, and I could heal some of my emotional wounds as I healed physically. And maybe, as I fixed the house, it would fix me too."

"Did it?"

"In a way it did. Working with your hands is very soothing, taking something that's terribly ugly and turning it into a masterpiece. I didn't have much skill beforehand, but I've been learning." He spoke with pride. "I'm about to put in a big deck outside. A veranda drifts down the front of the house with a big wide double staircase going up ten steps to the double front doors. But out in the back, there's nothing. It just drops off. I've put in French doors, but I haven't got a deck built yet."

"It sounds beautiful."

There was wonder in her tone. It made him smile.

"How many bedrooms?"

He dropped a kiss on her forehead, wondering where she was going with this. "There are four bedrooms."

She twisted to look up at him in surprise. "Why so big?"

He shrugged, not wanting to tell her.

"Because you wanted a family?" she asked, her tone low, gentle.

He nodded. "In the back of my mind, I was hoping, maybe one day, I would be blessed enough to find a woman who would take me as I am."

She pivoted in his arms and kissed him. "Well, there won't be *that* woman," she said in a determined voice. "So you can stop looking."

He looked at her in surprise, a core of dread forming in the stomach. "What do you mean?"

"I'm *that* woman. You found me already." Her smile was momentary as she kissed his nose and cheek.

He grabbed her and held her tight against him. "Do you mean that?"

"I've never meant anything more in my life. And I would never ask you to move here. I know you don't belong here in your heart, and honestly I don't anymore either. I was staying for my parents for some reason, and I don't know why. They aren't even here. They never come here. So what do they care? I could sell Chad's house, and, if you're agreeable"—she sat up, looking shy and uncertain—"I will move in with you."

He propped himself up too, his hand stroking the plump breast in front of him. "Are you sure you want to do that? So fast? We have only just reconnected."

"Yes." Her smile widened with joy. "I'm very sure. I'll turn in my two weeks' notice at work today. And we might have just reconnected, but, in reality, we never fully separated."

He stared at her in surprise. "Are you willing to give it all up? Chad's house? Although you could rent it out just to make sure, before you sell it outright. But what about your job here? What above your parents and their home? This was where you were born and where you've always lived."

"I can't do it anymore. It's all part of the same life I've lived for eight years. For way too long. A life that doesn't allow me to be me, doesn't let me laugh or smile. I don't really know anybody in the office because I don't socialize with anyone. Not at work and definitely not afterward. That's not what I did. I was this locked-down personality from morning 'til night. And I don't want that anymore. Since you've been here, I've laughed. I've cried. I've screamed. I've even hit you …" She frowned and stroked his cheek. "For that I'm so sorry."

He shook his head. "Hit away. I'm a big man, and your little blows are nothing for me."

"That may be, but it's still not right," she said regretfully. "But it's like the floodgates have opened. Yesterday I was bereft of everything. I didn't know who I was. I didn't know where I was. And some of those truths Jerry and I exchanged yesterday were very hard to assimilate. But I'm working on it. Last night was the best night I've had since you left," she admitted. "And this morning it's like so much of yesterday is over with. It'll take time, and I'll make mistakes. I might even lock down, tuck back into that little personality again every once in a while, but I'm sure you'll say something and pop me back out with the same fury I've seen these last couple days."

He watched her as she tried to sort out something that was important to say.

She glanced back at him and smiled. "I know it's weird to say, but it's like I've been in cold storage, until you came back. And I'm so damn grateful you did."

He pulled her into his arms and just held her.

Then she started to bawl.

He leaned down, brushed the tears off her cheeks and whispered, "And now why are you crying?"

She smiled through her tears and whispered, "Because I'm so happy."

He crushed her lips to his and made love to her with a ferocity that surprised them both. It was as if they were forging one soul from two broken spirits. If it were possible, then he would make sure it happened right now.

When it was over, they both lay exhausted, gasping for breath, holding on to each other for dear life. "I don't know what that was," she said, "but I want more. I want a lifetime of more."

He couldn't move to give her a kiss for that. He did manage to murmur, "You can have more. A lot more. But you'll have to wait and give me time to recover after this one. I think you just might kill me."

She sat up and looked at him. "Just like old times, huh? The good parts of the old times."

He grinned, his memories flooding his psyche. Because that's what they had been—hot, passionate lovers every time they made love.

She hopped off the bed, walking to the bathroom. He watched, his attention on her beautiful cheeks as she walked away from him. She called over her shoulder, "So, can you shower with those things on?" She stopped at the door, wearing a grin. "And, if you can, you better get your ass over here because I gotta be at work by nine. That means it's shower time now. And I know how much SEALs love the water."

CHAPTER 13

GETTING INTO HER vehicle later that morning was very difficult. She hated to leave Talon and Laszlo behind. While she had talked Talon out of coming to work with her, she suspected he was following her nonetheless. She had to smile thinking about that, how those two guys were more a part of her life than anybody else in it. She knew there was no way she would survive living in California while they were in Santa Fe. Trying to keep a long-distance relationship going with Talon wouldn't work. She'd lost Talon once because she hadn't been willing to give in. She had no intention of doing it again. Chad and Talon had been her life, and, when Talon had walked out, Chad had been her life. Her husband never took the top spot.

Once Chad was gone, she'd been so alone, missing the men who had been so important to her. Now that she had a chance to redo her relationship with Talon and make it bigger and better than it ever had been, she was desperate to make sure he didn't get a chance to change his mind. She knew he cared.

She hadn't yet told him how much she loved him. That oversight was something eating at her as she drove away from her house. She'd realized it when she was in the kitchen, waiting for the coffee to drip. And she hadn't found the right time after that.

She wasn't very far from her office. One of the first things she would do was hand in her letter of resignation. She wanted to talk to the manager and see if she could take her holidays due to her in lieu of working her last two weeks. She thought they owed her close to two weeks as it was. Might even be more. She'd signed a contract when she had first started with them but hadn't had a chance to double-check it at home to see how long a notice she was supposed to give.

She'd stay and work out what she needed to, but, if there was a chance to leave sooner, she'd turn around right now and head back home again. And it wouldn't take her long to handle what she needed to do to put Chad's house on the market. She had a friend in real estate. She'd be more than happy to take on the listing. There was no point in staying for Chad or her parents.

Her parents had made it very clear this wasn't their life. And Clary was welcome to join them as they traipsed around the backwoods of the world, but that so wasn't her life. Nor was staying in place in case somebody came home one day—not anymore anyway.

She pulled into the underground car park and hopped out.

Her boss got out of his vehicle a few spaces away from her. He waved and called out, "You look like you had a good weekend."

She winced. "I'm not sure that's true." She really liked him. He had always been kind. "And I do have some news that might be upsetting for you guys."

"Oh, what's that?" He walked closer to her as they spoke.

"I'm handing in my resignation today." As he was her

boss, she said, "This is verbal notice, and I'll follow it up with a written one too."

He stopped and shook his head. "I'm so sorry to hear that. I hope it's not a rival firm because we can always negotiate something to make you happier here." He frowned. "Honestly I didn't think you were unhappy here. Why are you leaving?"

She chuckled. "It has nothing to do with the job, nothing to do with the people. I'll be living in Santa Fe with somebody I should never have split with in the beginning."

A look of understanding crossed his face. "Aah, love. Well, that's an argument I can't win. If you're determined to go, then go with all our blessings."

She smiled. "Thank you. That is really nice." As she walked toward the elevators, she said, "I'm hoping to leave as soon as possible."

"Do you have any holidays coming?"

She nodded. "I do. And I cleaned off my desk pretty well last week."

He nodded. "I know the caseload right now is quite manageable. We'd have to hire somebody to replace you no matter what." His speech slowed as if thinking hard.

"You had two girls earlier this year for extra help. Emily, in particular, was really good. If you're looking for a replacement, I'd start with her."

He glanced at her in surprise. "I think I remember her—middle-aged, tall, no-nonsense attitude, very much a worker?"

Clary laughed. "That's her. She was *very* much a worker. She had everything organized and in tip-top shape like we've never seen it."

"In that case, I think we will give her a call. Why did we

let her go?"

"She was only in for holiday relief. Then we did manage to keep her for about four months as everybody went off on their vacations. But once your full-time staff was back, there wasn't enough work for her."

"Would you mind calling her, asking if she'd come in and talk to us, if she's interested in at least a temporary trial to see how it works out?"

"I can do that."

At the elevator, she realized she'd left her purse behind. She frowned and said, "Drat. I'm really ditsy this morning. I left my purse in the car." She started to walk back, turned, and said, "I'll be up in a few minutes." He waved at her, and she quickly retraced her steps to her car.

She unlocked it, bent in toward the passenger side, and pulled out her purse. As she straightened, slamming the door, she found a man with a baseball cap and a scarf, or something, pulled up to his chin in front of her. She frowned. "Can I help you?"

He smiled. "I'm sure you can." He bent down and clicked something around her legs before she had a chance to move.

She tried to take a step and fell down, crying out. "Help," she screamed.

The blow came out of nowhere, slamming against the side of her face. She moaned as a second blow was a direct hit against her jaw. She shuddered at the pain and felt herself being dragged on the concrete floor.

Struggling, she reached up and clawed at his hands gripped around her feet. If nothing else she'd have his DNA under her fingernails for somebody to nail this asshole.

But just the thought of that, just knowing there was a

chance she might not get that future she was so desperate to have with Talon, had her fighting like crazy. Kicking her feet free of his hands, she pulled her knees up to her chest. As he reached down again, she kicked him hard against his wrist.

He swore and started kicking her. She rolled and rolled again, trying to get away from him. But he was losing it, his blows getting harder and harder. There was a vehicle right beside her, and although it took more effort than she thought she had, she managed to slide underneath. He tried to catch her and pull her back out again. But a truck drove in.

He swore again, bent down, and snapped, "The next time I'll just shoot you." And he took off.

She waited until she heard his footsteps running away before she pulled her head out from underneath the vehicle. Her purse was lying beside her. She managed to get her cell phone out, quickly dialing Talon's number.

"Talon," she cried into the phone, her heart slamming against her chest as she frantically looked around to see if this asshole would come back. "I was just attacked in the parking lot where I work. Can you come get me?"

"Stay where you are. I'll be right there. I was just a couple blocks behind you."

Despite her shackled feet, she crawled to her vehicle, pulled herself inside, and locked the doors. She dropped the seat back until she was lying down, trying to hide. She could have called out for somebody else, but there was no way she would take the chance. She wanted Talon, and she wanted him now.

The sobs were threatening to break, but she didn't dare. She had to keep her wits about her. If this guy had seen her get back into her car, she was a sitting duck. She looked down at her feet and didn't understand what it was that he'd put on her. It was some kind of an instant locking mechanism was all she could tell. She stared at it and shuddered.

Her phone rang. "We're pulling into the parking lot. Where are you?"

"I'm inside my car," she said, crying now that she realized he was almost here. "Please find me."

Suddenly his face appeared in her driver's side window. She hit the Unlock button. He threw the door open and bent down, wrapping her in his arms. And she burst into sobs.

"Easy. You're okay now. It's all right."

She shook her head, shuddering in pain. "My feet," she stammered. "My feet."

He gave a strangled exclamation and carefully lifted her from the car. He tried to look at her feet but had to twist around so Laszlo could look instead.

Laszlo let out a light whistle. "Wow. I haven't seen one of these since our military days."

But the good news was, because he had seen them, he could also undo them. And just as suddenly as her legs had been tied up, she was free. She shifted her legs back and forth, making sure she could move. Talon, misunderstanding what she was doing, set her on her feet.

And she threw herself back into his arms. "I was walking to the elevator with my boss, but I forgot my purse," she cried out. "I came back to my car, grabbed my purse from the seat, turned around, and he was right there in front of me."

"Who?" His voice was hard, the look in his eyes deadly.

She shook her head. "He had on a baseball cap and a bandanna, a cowboy scarf, up over his nose. I couldn't see anything."

"Height?" Laszlo asked.

She turned to look at him. "Similar to you guys, but he was thinner. There was almost …" She stopped and thought about it. "Freckles. He had freckles on the back of his hands. He was dragging me by my feet in the parking lot here, and I managed to get one foot free. When he reached for me again, I kicked him really hard in the wrist, and he lost it. He started to kick the crap out of me," she said, crying again, shivering uncontrollably.

It took another few minutes before she could get more words out. "I just rolled, and kept rolling, hoping as I rolled, his blows would not be able to hit as hard. I made it under that vehicle beside us." She pointed to the truck.

"As he reached for me underneath there, I was screaming and screaming. Another vehicle drove in, and he told me the next time he would just shoot me."

At that she gave up and buried her face against Talon's chest and hugged him tight.

TALON JUST HELD her. The brazenness of the attack was unbelievable. That he'd used a military lock system for her feet was definitely concerning. He and Laszlo exchanged hard glances.

Laszlo walked around, looking for any evidence, something they could use to identify who the hell had been here. He called out, "Footprints over here."

He stood in a parking space beside the truck she'd rolled under. There had been some kind of leak, maybe antifreeze or coolant gathered underneath. The perpetrator had stepped in it, and his footsteps could be traced to a space on the opposite side of the car park. Laszlo followed the footprints as Talon watched and held her close.

"Hey, what's going on here?" a man roared behind him.

Talon turned to see a suited male racing toward them with anger, confusion, and concern on his face. He tilted Clary's face up and said, "Do you know him?"

"It's my boss."

He came to a stop beside them. "What happened, Clary?"

She sniffled. "I came back to get my purse, and I was attacked."

Talon took it from there and explained what had happened.

Her boss was horrified. "Have you called the police?"

She shook her head. "Not yet."

"You need to. Anybody see what vehicle he took off in?"

Clary shook her head. "Honestly I didn't see anything. Just his feet as he left."

"I know it's a long shot," Talon said, "but did you recognize what he was wearing?"

She closed her eyes as she thought about when she was fighting him off underneath the vehicle. "He had on jeans and some kind of work boots." She frowned, held up her hands. "I scratched his arm and neck to make sure, if I did end up dying, there'd be DNA."

Talon took a look of her fingers. "Good. We'll get this processed at a special lab."

She looked up at him. "How long will that take?"

"With enough money, not very long at all."

The lawyer said, "We'll pay for it. She was attacked in our building, and this is completely unacceptable."

Talon was gratified to see Clary's boss was, indeed, shimmering with rage. Talon glanced around. "Do you have cameras down here?"

The boss nodded, pulling out his phone. "I'm calling security. We'll get the video footage run. I also know a cop who has helped us out a couple times. I'll give him a quick call too." He looked at her. "How badly hurt are you?"

She gave him a wan smile. "I'm not exactly sure. He kicked me pretty hard. I haven't moved much yet, but I certainly hurt."

The boss turned to look at Talon. "And who are you?"

Talon's arms wrapped around her possessively, tucking her up close.

The boss nodded. "The reason why she told me this morning that she's quitting, I presume?"

Talon glanced at him in surprise.

"Yes, exactly," she said. "And I really don't want to go to work today."

Her boss snorted. "You're not only not working today but, as far as I'm concerned, the next few weeks will go under medical leave, then we'll pay out your vacation time. But I suggest you get to the hospital first and foremost to get checked out. It's too easy to have broken a rib if he had work boots on. Those steel toes can cause all kinds of damage."

Talon agreed. He looked down at her. "Do you need anything from here? Anything personal from your office or your car?"

She shook her head. "No, my desk was clean. There's nothing I need to worry about here."

Talon glanced over at her boss. "Does she need to sign anything?"

The lawyer shook his head. "We can send it by email.

Get her to the hospital. And make sure you protect her. Plus get those fingernails processed. I want this asshole prosecuted." And with that, he stormed off, still on his phone.

Talon reached out a gentle hand and stroked Clary's cheek. "I'm so sorry this happened to you, honey."

She nodded.

Talon helped her into the passenger side of her car. "Let me talk to Laszlo for a moment, and then I'll take you to the hospital."

"I probably don't need the hospital, just a clinic."

He wasn't so sure about that but wasn't prepared to argue. Her boss was already walking back inside, his stride hard, angry. Talon was glad he appeared to be a good man, had looked after Clary for so long.

Laszlo reached Talon just as he walked out to the end of the car park. "No sign of anyone here."

Talon brought him up to speed on what the boss had said.

Laszlo nodded. "You go get her checked out. I'll stay here and talk to security, see if we can come up with something on the video feed."

"He had jeans on and work boots. Tall, slim. She said he had freckles on his hands."

"So maybe a redhead? Light-haired, definitely Caucasian."

With that Talon walked back to Clary. He hopped into the vehicle. "The hospital is better if you think you've got busted ribs. If we're likely to be looking at just bruises and cuts, then the clinic will work."

She sighed. "The clinic might be faster."

He made an executive decision and said, "Any good doctor will send you for X-rays anyway, so we'll start at the hospital."

She sagged back in place.

Once he got her in the emergency room, they told the triage nurse what had happened. They were told to take a seat but luckily only had to wait twenty minutes.

She got sorer and stiffer the longer she sat. When she stood up again, she gasped as the pain stabbed into her side and her head throbbed. One hand went to her side and the other to her head as she cried out.

Talon helped her into the cubicle, and they waited for somebody to come and check her out.

When the nurse came in, Talon looked at Clary and asked, "Do you want me to stay, or do you want me to go?"

She said, "Stay."

And what followed was an hour of examination, nails clipped for DNA collection, doctor consult, and then off to the X-ray department. As he suspected, the doctor wanted to check out some of the bruises and swelling taking over her body. When she had to strip down for the doctor to see how bad the damage was, it had been all Talon could do to hold back his own cries of fury at the damage this asshole had inflicted on her.

Back from the X-rays, they had to wait again for the radiologist to look at them and then for the doctor to speak with her once more. Talon had had several text messages from Laszlo. He'd sent out notices to everybody in the group to let them know what had happened. This wasn't the way anybody wanted anything to end.

The good news was, she didn't have to go back to her job. And, for that, Talon was grateful. He fully planned to return to Santa Fe with her. He just may have to delay their trip until she could handle the traveling without additional pain.

CHAPTER 14

BY THE TIME she made it home, Clary was stiff and sore; every movement made her want to cry. She waited in the car until Talon raced around to her side to help her out. She had two cracked ribs, a bruised spleen, intestinal bruises, and more spots than she could count that just plain hurt. Her attacker hadn't broken her arm, even though she'd taken a direct hit on it. It looked pretty ugly though. And the ribs, the doctor told her, would heal. She just had to take it easy and give them time.

Easier said than done, given her current circumstances. But at least she didn't have to return to work. And apparently her boss was doing everything he could to help find who attacked her. It felt good to have people on her side.

Maybe she hadn't been alone all this time. Maybe she'd just felt she had deserved to be alone.

She wanted to go into the living room and sit down, but Talon wasn't listening to her. He ushered her upstairs and straight to bed. She had to admit, as soon as she managed to relax in a semiprone position, her body settling into the soft comforter, he was right.

He returned with a couple painkillers and a glass of water. "The doctor said two every four hours for the rest of today."

Grateful, she swallowed them.

He grabbed a blanket and gently placed it over her. "I'd love it if you would sleep, so your body can heal, but, if you're not ready to sleep, is there anything I can get you?"

"No, sleep is probably the best thing." As he started to walk away, she called out to him, hating to hear the tremor in her voice. "Where are you going?"

He turned and walked back to the bed. "How about I get my laptop from downstairs, and I'll come sit on the bed. We can talk until you can sleep."

She smiled at him gratefully. "That sounds good."

As he went back to the door, he asked, "Do you want some coffee? I can put on a pot while I'm downstairs."

"Sure," she said quietly. "I'll probably stay awake long enough for that." She smiled as he disappeared downstairs. She'd always considered herself a strong independent female, but there was a lot to be said for having someone take care of her.

In contrast her marriage had been more of a business relationship, now that she looked at it. They had had separate bank accounts and, in a way, even separate furniture, as he hadn't liked her choices, nor she his. Although, when she had moved out, she'd left everything behind because she was moving into her and Chad's house, which was already furnished.

Talon returned a few minutes later, carrying two full cups of coffee, his laptop tucked under one arm. Setting everything on the bedside table, he gently eased himself on the bed so as not to jostle her, leaning over to drop a soft kiss on her temple. "How are you feeling now?"

"A little bit better," she admitted. "I ache in spots I didn't even know existed."

"You took quite a beating." His tone was hard. "You can

bet he'll get his."

"I just want him to stop," she whispered.

"Any chance it's the MacArthur guy?"

"Maybe." She lay there with her eyes closed, trying to relive what she had seen. From a distance, the fear wasn't quite so extreme. But she must have given her thoughts away because he reached down and gently stroked her shoulder.

"I'm not asking you to delve too deeply into that memory, but you must have gotten an impression of him."

She thought about that for a few moments. "It's possible. He had the same build."

"Good enough."

"What about the DNA?" she asked.

"We got it from you, although you probably don't remember."

She glanced down at her nails and realized they'd all been clipped. Not even so much cleaned out as clipped. "Good thing I'm not the kind to fuss about my nails."

"I didn't do too bad a job, did I?" he protested.

She smiled. "No. You can give me a manicure anytime." She rolled over slowly so she was facing him, wincing as her body screamed in protest. When she could look at him again, he studied her with concern. She smiled. "I'm fine." She knew her voice was drowsy, but every time she thought that maybe she could just relax and fall asleep, memories danced into her head and brought her back out again. "What do you want to talk about?" She would try to keep up her end of the conversation.

"You really quit your job today?"

"I really did."

"Are you really serious about moving to Santa Fe with me?"

"I'm really serious."

"You have a life here," he said quietly. "I don't want to take that away from you."

"No, I don't have a life here. You and Chad were my life. I lost you, and then I lost Chad. If I have you back again, I'm not letting you go." She glared at him. "Stop trying to get out of it."

He raised his eyebrows and stared at her. "I just want you to be sure."

Her eyes drifted closed. "I'm sure."

"And Chad's house?"

"A friend of mine is a Realtor. When I'm feeling better, I'll give her a call and have her come by. She'll get an assessor out to give us a fair market value. Then I'll have her put it on the market."

"It's a pretty fast decision," he cautioned. "You could wait to make a decision on it for a while. Leave it empty if you wanted or rent it."

"No, it's not what Chad would want either. It's time for me to move on."

She could sense his calmness as she lay here. "It's not the first time I've thought about it," she said. "After Chad died, I didn't know what to do. I told myself that I'd give it a year. Well, I've given it a year, and now I have a reason to make a change. So I think we should make that change happen," she said brightly.

"And the furniture?"

"I guess if there's anything we want to move to Santa Fe, we'd have to look at the logistics of doing that. Otherwise, what does one do when they have an entire houseful of furnishings to get rid of?"

"Well, there's probably some charity that would come in

and take whatever they could use. It's also possible to sell the house as is, so all the furniture goes with it."

She thought about that. "That's not a bad idea. We could just take a few pieces we wanted, for Chad's sake, and leave the rest for somebody else."

"Talk to your friend in the real estate business about the issue."

"I can do that."

"What will you do when you get to Santa Fe?"

"Nothing," she said promptly.

He chuckled. "That was a really fast answer."

"It's a very fast answer but a well-thought-out response. I would really like to have a break for a while. It's been a pretty tough couple years. Santa Fe will be different. I want time to adjust and to figure out my next step. Maybe return to my art. Full-time this go-round."

"You might not need to do anything," he said. "This house will get you a lot of money. If it's invested, you'll have a decent income from it."

"That's fine. I'm not sure how I feel about being a housewife." Her words slipped out as she yawned, the sound loud as the stress started to waste away, and the drugs took over. "But you know I'm always willing to try new things. So that could work out really well." She yawned again a second time and murmured, "I can't keep my eyes open."

"Sleep," he said gently. "It's what your body needs."

She reached out a hand, instinctively looking for that security of knowing he was there. When his fingers closed around hers, she let the last of her restraints fall away and allowed sleep to claim her.

HOUSEWIFE, HUH?

Talon grinned at the sleeping beauty beside him. Sleeping beauty, except for the tear-stained cheeks and the visible bruises. But he wouldn't think about that right now. He was so damn glad she had survived her attack. And he really liked the idea of her moving in with him. His house was huge, and though there was a lot of work still to be done, there was no rush to finish the upgrades. The house was very livable as is.

And neither was there a rush for her to find a job. This house would be an astronomical sale. And with that kind of money, she didn't have to do anything, maybe ever again. He was happy for her. This way, if she did decide to do something, he hoped it would be more of her artwork. She was incredibly talented. This was a good time for her to resume her craft.

He settled back to work on the emails flying into his inbox and to catch up on the news. It would take days, if not a week, to get DNA results, even with a rush put on it and extra fees paid. That wouldn't help them right now. He was more concerned about the asshole's threat that he would just shoot her next time. Because that was too easy.

His phone buzzed. He pulled it out to see a text from Laszlo.

Call me if you can.

Talon hit Talk and waited until the call went through. "What have you found out?"

"First, how is she?"

"Two cracked ribs and multiple bruises. Some intestinal bruising, including her spleen and liver. She'll be a bit of a mess for the next few days." He spoke quietly so as not to wake her. "We're in her room. She's sleeping right now."

"Good. The video cameras did show a black Porsche

came in," Laszlo said. "It dropped somebody off, but, when the guy took off, it was in a blue Audi."

"So," Talon continued, "we have two vehicles currently in play in San Diego, the blue Audi and the black Porsche. The asshole who attacked Clary was dropped off by whoever was driving the black Porsche and expected to take the Audi out of there."

"Yes," Laszlo said. "The cameras caught him coming in and waiting to nab her, but she saw her boss right away. Then she came back for her purse, and the boss goes on into the offices, and the guy nabs her then. What he did to her is all there on the video too."

"Good, we'll need it for the court case."

"Or he might accidentally not make it to the courts." Laszlo's voice was hard. "I saw him beat the crap out of her. If another vehicle hadn't come in just then, I don't know what he would have done to her."

"A hair-trigger temper?"

"Yes, definitely. It wasn't too bad, then, all of a sudden, when she hurt him, he just lost it."

"Any chance of getting a facial ID on him?"

"The cops have seen the video as well. One of them seems to think he knows who the guy is. He's trying to find the name now, and we're sending the images out to all stations to get a BOLO out on him."

"As long as they're on the lookout for this guy and pick him up and understand he's armed and dangerous, then it's all good." There was silence on the phone for a moment, then Talon asked, "What do you think his next move will be?"

"Honestly? I think he'll make an attempt on the house."

Talon agreed. "Better come back here then. I might need

some backup."

"You don't know it, but I'm already here." Laszlo chuckled. "I'm in the back, hiding behind the fences while I talk to you. I'll do a scout around. Make sure there's no Audi parked within a couple blocks of here. Watch your back. She's already taken a huge beating. Any more could put her out permanently."

Talon hung up and thought about that. This guy could get into the house either with keys or through the windows, and there wasn't a whole lot Talon could do about it. Not in a house this big with minimal security features. He was one person. He couldn't watch every entrance. So, what he really needed to do was make sure he could defend them. Laszlo was doing a search outside and would slowly narrow that perimeter down. But, unless Talon could get a warning off to Laszlo in time, there wouldn't be any backup coming to help Talon and Clary.

Just then he thought he heard something in the kitchen. He hopped off the bed and headed to the bedroom door to listen. He pulled out his phone and sent Laszlo a quick text.

Intruder in the house now?

Can't see anything.

Downstairs, kitchen.

Coming around.

Talon glanced around the bedroom, looking for a place to hide. It was obvious this guy would be coming up to the master bedroom because that's where Clary was. Talon could hide behind the door, but that was hardly ideal. What he didn't want to do was have this guy open the door and fire a shot at Clary.

Just then there was a creak on the stairs.

He swore silently and sent another message to Laszlo,

stepping well behind the door so the intruder couldn't flatten him with it. He reached down and pulled a knife from his prosthetic leg that he had temporarily placed there. He had planned to talk to Kat about something permanent. But he'd take what he could right now. At least he had a weapon.

The door opened only four inches. He waited, cantering himself, knowing what would happen next. He kept his eye on the door's edge. The gunman would have to open it farther to line up his shot with the bed.

But there was no way in hell he would get a shot off. Not while Talon was here. He waited and nothing happened. He had his phone in his hand, checking for messages from Laszlo. Then he heard another sound downstairs. He froze. Had the intruder gone back down, or was that Laszlo coming back? Shit. What he didn't want was to have the intruder go after Laszlo.

Just then the door was nudged ever-so-slightly. And damn it if the tip of a gun barrel didn't come slowly around the corner. Clary was still out of the line of fire, but Talon needed more of the gun to appear, more of the gun for him to grab, so he waited.

The door opened slightly more. It was enough that the gun lined up on the woman of Talon's heart, and he jumped. With his prosthetic hand, he grabbed the weapon and ripped it out of the man's hand. Yanking the man's arm, Talon slammed the door shut hard against his forearm. The man groaned on the other side.

But Talon had the door open again and was already kicking the gunman. He heard a commotion downstairs, but he was so focused on pounding this asshole's face into the ground that he didn't hear the shouts or the cries.

The man beneath him stopped moving. Talon stopped

and leaned back for a moment to assess.

He checked and confirmed the gunman was unconscious. It was MacArthur.

There were still sounds of a fight downstairs, and he realized MacArthur hadn't come alone. He took the man's belt from around his waist and made quick work of tying his hands behind his back. Then he restrained the man's feet by tying his shoelaces behind his back and then to his hands. When he was sure the gunman wasn't a further danger to Clary, he dragged him to the top of the stairs.

With the gun in his hand, he slipped down to the first landing. He took a look around the corner to see Laszlo fighting hard. He raced into the room, and a shot rang out.

Talon placed the gun to the intruder's head. "Stop."

Slowly Laszlo, breathing hard, straightened and slammed his fist into the gunman's chin. The man groaned and slid to his knees before falling over sideways. Laszlo ripped the gun out of the man's hand.

Talon looked at him. "Are you hit?"

Laszlo shook his head. "No, no, I'm fine." He bent over for a moment to catch his breath and motioned at the intruder. "There were two of them?"

"It was always a possibility, but we figured there was only one trigger man at this point. I've got the second one upstairs." Talon reached over and pulled the guy's scarf off the lower part of his face and the baseball cap off his head. And he stopped and stared. "Who the hell's this guy?"

Laszlo reached down and pulled the man's shirt away from his neck and upper arms. "This is the asshole who attacked Clary."

Her scratches, her fight for her life, were obvious on his body. As were the freckles she'd seen …

Talon shot Laszlo a hard look. "I'll go retrieve the other one so we have them both in the same place. I really want to just beat this guy into the ground, like he beat her. But I think I like the idea of him in a cage better."

He stepped over the prone man and headed upstairs. Thankfully the man he'd taken out was still unconscious. He pulled him around and dragged him downstairs to where Laszlo stood over the other man. With both of the men together, they took pictures of their faces and injuries while they tried to identify what the hell was going on, who the second man was, and why he along with MacArthur were after Clary.

"Do you get the feeling these two were just hired thugs?"

"You mean, the theory that we're being played? That somebody is putting all this into motion just to get to us? Oh, yeah."

Having called the cops and gathering the two men still unconscious at his feet, Talon said, "I'll go check on Clary."

He took the stairs two at a time, hating that sick feeling in his stomach at how close these assholes had come. If he and Laszlo hadn't been here, he knew for sure Clary would be dead. Even knowing they had the two men secured, his stomach was still knotted as he pushed the door open and checked on her. She continued to sleep soundly.

He walked through the room just to make sure it was safe. Walking over to the balcony, he stepped out. A shadow was his only warning.

Instinctively he threw up his arm to ward off the blow that came out of nowhere. He fell to his knees as he tried to roar a scream of warning for Laszlo. But a second chop to his throat had him falling backward, almost incapable of making a sound. He reached for the gunman's arm twisting, pulling, fighting—not only for his life but for Clary's. And a hard fight it was.

A scream ripped through the air from behind him. He didn't know what she had used to hit the gunman with, but he stood there for a long moment bending over sideways, as if trying to recover from the blow. And then in a move that startled them both, he jumped over the balcony railing to the bushes below.

Talon moved to jump after him, but Clary cried out, "No."

He stopped and looked at her in confusion. That's when she said, "You've been shot."

He stared at her, and then the pain hit. He swore but could hear Laszlo yelling from down below.

"I'm on him."

Relieved to think maybe this guy wouldn't get away, he placed the towel Clary had raced to get over the hole in the shoulder of his good arm. "I have to go downstairs. We have two men unconscious. I can't take the chance of either of them getting away."

"I'm coming with you," Clary said, "and you have to go carefully."

He headed down the stairs, swearing as every step jarred his wound. He was angrier at himself for having gotten shot and not having caught the goddamn third man. And there was something about that confrontation that bothered him. But he didn't get a chance to say anything. Hearing a noise in the kitchen, he froze, sliding her behind him protectively and out of the way.

He peered around the corner of the kitchen but saw nothing, nobody. Keeping her with him, he raced through the kitchen and around to the other side where it looped to the dining room and back around to the living room again. As they crossed to the dining room, he heard two hard spits. Gunfire. Blood splatted the wall in front of him. Making sure Clary stayed out of sight, he raced to the living room window to see a man jumping into a blue car and disappearing.

He turned around to see Clary, staring. She cried out, "Did he double back inside the house? He killed them."

Talon rushed over, and, sure enough, both gunmen sported a bullet in their foreheads.

"Where's Laszlo?" she demanded.

"He went after him."

A door slammed behind them, and Laszlo raced toward them from the kitchen. "I lost him," Laszlo seethed.

"That's because he snuck around and came back inside. He shot our two intruders," Talon snapped. "And I missed him too."

Grim, the two men stared at each other.

"So this isn't over, is it?" Clary cried out, staring at the two of them.

Talon turned to look at her. She was swaying against the doorjamb. Her body had already taken too much abuse for the day. But he knew it would be a longer day yet. They had the police to deal with, and he had a bullet hole to get stitched up.

"No, it's not." He shook his head. "But it's over for the moment."

CHAPTER 15

CLARY STAYED AT Talon's side. When the police arrived only minutes after they'd lost their third gunman, the officers sent men out looking for the blue Audi. The detective stayed, getting their statements.

Talon refused to go to the hospital until everything was cleaned up. And then he let Laszlo drive him. Clary refused to stay home and wait and was shocked when he refused to have general anesthesia. The doctors wanted him to go in for surgery to get the bullet removed, but he was pretty stone-faced when he said, "It's not that deep. Just pull it out." The doctor tried to talk him out of it, but Talon said, "No general anesthetics—just get it done and then I'm out of here."

Finally the doctor gave in and said, "It's your funeral."

But they hadn't had the primer on pain that Talon apparently had.

Clary had protested his decision too, then gave up as she saw how adamant he was about it. She stood outside after they gave him a local and prepared to take out the bullet.

She listened to the doctor as he completed the job. "Aha, there it is. Now just a few moments to stitch this up, and you'll be as good as new." Soon afterward, the doctor said, "Let's get this bandaged. Keep it dry, and get to your doctor in twenty-four hours to get it checked over."

"Thanks."

She stepped into the room in stunned amazement to see him stand and walk toward her—in obvious pain but, just as obviously, he was determined not to show it.

In a low voice, she asked, "Are you okay?"

He gave a grim nod. "But we'll be sharing the painkillers for a while."

"We'll get your prescription filled."

"No need. If we need more, we can get them tomorrow. I'd like to go home and get to bed. They did give me a pain shot, so that will hold me for a few hours."

He was walking at a steady clip, but she had no idea for how long. The fresh air helped them both feel a little better. At the parking lot, Laszlo helped him get into the car; then Laszlo drove them back home. The day was wearing on her. She couldn't think of anything she'd like more than to go to bed and sleep.

"You should have let them check you in for the night."

"The only time I will be staying overnight in a hospital again is when I'm in the morgue."

She shot him a look. "Were the hospital visits that bad?"

He didn't answer.

She figured that was his answer already. "I wish I'd stayed beside you when they pulled out the bullet."

"No, it's better that you weren't."

"Why? Why do you have to be so tough all the time?"

"It would have been harder on me if you were there."

She glanced at him as they pulled into the driveway. "How does that make any sense?"

"Every time I see your bruised face, I just get angrier that I wasn't able to stop this asshole."

"We'll get the guy behind all this," she said gently.

They had been at the hospital about six hours this trip. Knowing Talon had refused to go in for surgery had almost broken her. But when the doctors had agreed to just pull the bullet out, she'd had to walk out of there. And, of course, he'd wanted her gone too. She didn't understand that but wondered if he didn't want her to see him at his weakest point.

However, he got treated; they were both home now; the police were still inside the house, taking measurements and photographs.

Laszlo said, "I suggest both of you take knockout pills and go lie down. But maybe food first?" He had a spatula in hand and aimed it at the kitchen.

The two of them, holding on to each other, battle weary after a war hard-fought, sat down as Laszlo delivered first hot coffee, then not long afterward hefty steak sandwiches to both of them.

Talon looked at Laszlo. "What about you?"

Laszlo pointed to the pan. "Mine is coming."

"Did the police have anything to add?" Clary asked, her voice barely holding up. The food did look good, though she was so exhausted that she couldn't imagine eating even half of it. She cut into her steak sandwich and took a bite. She chewed, enjoying having a meal prepared for her.

Laszlo answered her question. "The man you knew as MacArthur was a con man. The other man was his buddy. At this point we figure the Porsche driver was the one who hired them."

"So once again we're a step behind."

"Yes, and no," Laszlo said. "We almost caught him this time. He's got to be getting nervous because we're right on his ass."

"But now he'll go underground," Talon said, "and we won't find him again until he chooses to resurface."

"Did you remember whatever it was that was bothering you about him?"

"I can barely even think. The shot is taking effect," Talon said. "I'm hoping to remember it once I stop worrying about it."

"Good enough."

The two finished eating in silence as Laszlo joined them. Talon looked at him and said, "Are you hurt?"

Laszlo shook his head. "I'm fine. You guys go to bed. I'll stand watch."

"But you stood watch all last night."

"I got a couple hours off and on."

Clary turned to look at Laszlo, hating the fear surging back into her gut. "Do you think he'll come back tonight?"

"No. This guy is a coward. You realize he keeps hiring other people to do his dirty work, then takes them out before his hired guns can talk. He's taken off. He'll lie low and figure out his next plan. So will we. I want both of you to go up to bed and just sleep. We'll talk in the morning."

It wasn't very late, but they were both so exhausted that neither argued. Holding on to each other, they made their way upstairs to the master bedroom.

While Clary walked to the bed and stripped down, crawling in nude, Talon headed to the balcony, where he'd lost sight of the asshole who'd been waiting for him. As he stood, he realized the tree was close enough for anybody adept enough to climb up the tree to the balcony. He shook his head. "So goddamn close."

He turned and closed the door, locking it, then walked to the bed and sat down.

"I never even thought about how it's your good arm that got shot," Clary whispered as she slowly stood and went around the bed to help him undress. "I doubt that was accidental …"

"Yeah, that'll be a bit of a bitch for a while."

Slowly he stripped down and crawled into bed, collapsing. She walked to the other side and got in beside him. Curled up together, both exhausted, they crashed.

TALON WOKE TO the sound of birds singing outside on the balcony. He sat up, slipped out of bed, wincing at the movement, used the bathroom, took a look at his wound, and shrugged. "I've seen worse," he said to the mirror.

He made his way over to the glass balcony doors and took another look outside. Even though he could see the tree and understood how the intruder had snuck in, it still pissed him off. He hadn't expected a third man.

Hell, they hadn't really expected the second one. He turned, walked back to the bed, and sat down beside the still-sleeping Clary. And that's when it hit him. He got back up again, walked over to the glass doors, and stopped. In his mind he replayed the fight and saw something he hadn't expected to ever see again. A tattoo. A large one on the man's neck. Somehow, in the fight, the bandanna he'd tied below his eyes had fallen off.

He'd been clean-shaven, and Talon had never really had a chance to see his face clearly, but he remembered seeing a large peripheral mark on the man's neck down the shoulder. He'd kept it mostly hidden by a collared shirt and a T-shirt underneath.

And this man had worn a winter wool cap that had come low and snug over his head. But Talon had seen the mark before. He was sure he'd seen it.

Leaving Clary to sleep, he pulled on a pair of sweatpants he used for running and a loose muscle shirt. He made his way downstairs. Laszlo sat at the kitchen table.

"I wasn't expecting to see you this early," he said in surprise. "How are you feeling?"

"Like someone tried to turn me into hamburger."

Laszlo nodded sympathetically. He got up and poured Talon a cup of coffee.

"I remembered what it was that was bothering me. I just figured it out this morning," Talon said quietly. "Only I don't understand what I saw."

"Tell me."

"He had a mark I recognized. Or think I did."

"Who?"

Talon turned to look at him directly. He spread his fingers apart to show the size of the tattoo and then pointed to the location of the mark down low on his neck. "The third guy. I couldn't see it clearly and had no time to confirm it, but it was right here."

Laszlo stared at him, looked at the place he'd pointed out, and then glanced back at his face. And then it hit him. His gaze widened, and his jaw dropped. "Mouse had a mark like that."

Talon nodded slowly. "Exactly."

"You're not thinking it's Mouse back from the dead, are you?"

Talon shook his head. "No. But I'm wondering if somebody didn't get a matching tattoo to make us think that. Or because he was honoring Mouse."

"What it does do," Laszlo said in a hard voice, "is cement the idea that this nightmare really surrounds Mouse."

"Clary was right," Talon said quietly. "I just wish to God we were a little further into this investigation."

"Are you staying here?"

He looked around the room. "No, not necessarily. She wants to move to Santa Fe with me."

Laszlo nodded as if just confirming what he already thought. "How quickly?"

"She handed in her notice at work yesterday. And given what happened in the parking lot, they're basically letting her use sick leave as her time remaining, and then they'll pay out her vacation time. I have to admit her boss was decent."

Laszlo smiled. "Nice to know some good guys are out there."

"Lots of good guys are in my house right now," Clary said cheerfully as she slowly walked into the kitchen, wearing a long robe. She poured herself a cup before joining the men at the table. "Although I feel like shit, I do feel better than I did yesterday."

"You should still be in bed," Talon snapped at her.

"Only if you are," she said, lifting her coffee cup to take a sip. "You don't look much better than I feel."

He shrugged and then winced.

"So, are you guys planning out the next step?" she asked in a conversational tone.

"It's time to go home," Laszlo said. "I have a meeting with the rest of the guys, and we'll figure out what our next step is."

"Good. Am I welcome to join you?"

Laszlo studied her for a long moment. "Are you moving in with Talon?"

"I am. And we can't leave soon enough." She fished her phone out of her pocket and looked down at it. "In fact, my Realtor friend will be here in ninety minutes."

"It's awfully fast," Talon warned. "I told you not to make a decision—"

"It's not fast. And I told you that already," she interrupted him. "What I have to decide is what is here that I want to keep, if anything, and what to do with the rest of it."

"It sounds like you've already made up your mind," Laszlo said.

Talon watched her, seeing no sense of indecision on her face.

She smiled and said, "Absolutely and grateful for it." She reached across and covered Talon's fingers with her own. "We've wasted enough time."

"I can't argue with that," Talon said. "I just want to make sure you're certain."

She leaned over, kissed him gently on the temple, and said, "I'm sure. Santa Fe, here we come."

"Forever?" he asked, a slight edge to his tone.

She sat down in the chair next to him and looked at him. "Forever," she said firmly. "No way in hell am I letting you go raring off after this guy if I'm not there with you."

He raised an eyebrow and studied her.

And she beamed. "You can look all you want. You can be distrustful for as long as you need to be. But, at some point, you'll realize how much I love you and how I always have. I've changed, finally grown up. I know what I want, and what I want is you."

He leaned over and kissed her. A kiss of promise. A kiss of forever. But most of all, a kiss of love and respect.

EPILOGUE

LASZLO JENSEN WATCHED as Talon, his good arm bandaged, and Clary, her face sporting colorful bruises, walked into Badger's house. Clary was shy, standing almost as if a part of Talon. Like everybody would already know and judge her for their past.

Dotty, Badger's coonhound, accepted Clary as is, wagging her tail furiously and walking up to greet each visitor, which is how Dotty greeted everyone. Clary laughed, broke away from Talon, squatting gently to give the sweet dog a cuddle.

When she stood up again, Badger stepped forward on his crutches and said, "There you are."

Clary smiled and reached up and gave him a hug. He hugged her back gently. Talon hadn't shared much about her past, but Badger didn't need to know to understand how hard it was to heal from what she'd been through. But since she'd moved into Talon's, the two of them had had lots of time to work through their old differences and to get comfortable being in the same space again. And now it was as if they'd never been apart.

With everyone seated in the living room of Badger's house, Laszlo settled back, loving the feeling of having his friends grow in number and become a bigger, stronger family than even what they were before. Badger was moving, though slowly. It would be a long time before he would get his prosthetic back. Kat, at his side always, doted on him.

Laszlo knew they would have some badass prosthetics coming their way, when the time was right. And he couldn't wait. He glanced around at the group and said, "It's good to see everybody back here again."

"Except not everybody's here," Erick said. "Jager's missing. He's still dark."

"Do we know for sure he's even alive?"

Erick nodded. "I got another message. But it was simple. He's still hunting."

"He always was a bit of a loner," Laszlo said. "If he'd at least check in with us, we'd have a chance to tell him what information we have."

"Speaking of information"—Geir sat on the far side of the room—"Jager's a good man. And, when he's hunting, there's no one else like him. But I wish to hell I was out there hunting with him."

Erick nodded. "And we're all here today to figure out what should happen next—and for Badger's sake. As he's not supposed to be moving as much as he is right now."

Badger waved his arm. "I'm fine."

Kat reached over and laced her fingers with his.

Laszlo smiled. "With Kat at your side, it's no wonder you're fine."

There was some good-humored ribbing, which Badger accepted with a smile. "She's the best thing that's happened to me." His gaze locked on Laszlo. "Did you ever notice the similarity between our group and Mason's and Levi's?"

Laszlo winced. "Hell no."

Erick and Talon chuckled. "Well, you should. Because you're next."

Cade had stayed quiet in the corner, Faith at his side, a couple beers open between the two of them. "It's all right, Laszlo. When you're ready, it'll happen."

Laszlo shook his head. "What I'm ready for is to find this asshole."

"That's why we're gathered together," Erick began. "We've got several threads to pull, and they are not in any particular order. And, Badger, chime in if I've forgotten anything or have my wires crossed here."

Badger nodded, patting Dotty, sitting by his chair.

"As you all know, our Afghanistan explosion was not an accident. We believe a US military-grade land mine was buried and used to explode our truck. Plus thereafter we've lost seven family members in vehicular deaths posing as accidents. Laszlo's father too was a victim of a hit-and-run, but he lived to tell the tale. So the guy we're after, the guy behind all the hit men and the hired guns and the snipers seems to be killing off his minions, like John Smith is dead, John MacArthur is dead, the unnamed man who attacked Clary is dead. Of course Badger killed the sniper who killed our first informant Ben Chambers.

"I'm in touch with Mason and Levi daily, sharing intel, and yet we haven't found out much as to our dead hired guns. So let's pull what threads we've got and see where they go. Here's the first." Erick pointed his pen at Cade and Faith. "Faith saw US dog tags on John Smith, our now-dead hit man who owned and drove the black Lexus, yet he was last seen here in Santa Fe but also in San Diego about fourteen months ago. He's taken responsibility for the deaths of Cade's sister and Talon's friend and Clary's brother Chad, plus the hit-and-run on Laszlo's father that left him incapacitated but alive."

Cade booted up his laptop. "I'll have Faith look at the different dog tags online. We'll see if we can narrow that down now."

"Great. Talon, while I'm thinking about this, I understand you're following up at your hospital in San Diego on who told you about Chad's death."

Talon nodded. "I did but that went nowhere. The feeds are missing, no longer available."

Erick nodded. "Figures. Kat, can you hook us up with a printer in case we need one?"

Kat stood. "I'm on it."

Badger smiled. "She's even beginning to talk like us." Everyone in the room could see how proud he was of her.

"Plus," Erick said, "did we have anybody canvass the San Diego city cameras to follow the black Porsche and the blue Audi before and after the attack on Clary? Granted, Clary's attacker himself is dead, who was seen driving the blue Audi, but so is John MacArthur, the registered owner of that blue Audi. However, someone drove away in the black Porsche, after dropping off Clary's attacker in her parking lot at work. Whoever he is, he may have a hidey-hole in California."

Talon gave a quick chin nod. "Let me work that angle. I think Clary's boss, as an attorney, might get us some special privileges there with the cops, being a local."

"Done." Erick ran a finger over one of his two notebooks. "Okay, for clarity, we had John Smith's black Lexus and the money man's rented BMW involved here in Santa Fe. But John Smith is dead, so his black Lexus is not on our radar anymore. And Warren Watson was renting the BMW but has since gone home. Again not on our radar at this time. But that small hatchback got away with our gunman inside at the airport after he failed to kill the money man.

But I have to ask, Why so many men? So many vehicles?"

"Misdirection," Talon said with confidence.

"A red herring," Laszlo said. "Fitting for the game this SOB thinks he's playing."

"But there was something about our money man that bothered me." Erick checked one of his notebooks. "Here it is. Per a run of the rental car plates—and I guess from the name he gave at the counter—he's supposedly ex-military, *as in American*, guys and gals. He's a former supply clerk, dishonorably discharged due to suspicion of stealing, among other things, land mines. Which should raise red flags for all of us. But I'm confused as to why he would use his real name in his line of business. Or why he would use a fake name that led us to a crooked supply clerk? I thought we were running his photo ID too, from his DL given when he rented the BMW. Again to confirm the name. But I haven't got that back either. This is such a jumbled mess and makes no logical sense to me. I suggest we start with someone asking Mason to run a search on *dishonorably discharged supply clerks*. How many could there be over the last five, ten years?"

Clary spoke up. "Let me take care of that." When everybody stared, Talon smiled at her and squeezed her hand. She sat taller, and smiled at him. "I'm in between jobs right now. You seem to be using Levi and Mason, predominantly, other than the local police departments. Let me see what I can find out for you."

"Great. Thanks, Clary. Talon can give you the telephone numbers, emails, whatever you need." Erick wrote something quickly in his notebook.

At that point, Kat returned with a printer and set it up nearby.

Erick said, "Thanks, Kat. Next is Monkeyman, a possible American, along with his two companions, Dumbo and the bald ex-fighter, who Honey had the displeasure of meeting in Afghanistan for her dental conference. Now Cade and Laszlo and I all were there for Monkeyman's building-climbing feats. But, Talon, could this be your guy on Clary's balcony? Granted, not as impressive, but Monkeyman got away from us in Afghanistan. We have yet to ID him. Yet again we have to consider that he was an American, possibly in the military, who possesses special skills." Erick turned to Talon, all eyes on him.

"The guy climbing on Clary's second-story balcony had a neck tattoo. It was similar to the one Mouse had, in the same location. I can tug that line, pass off anything I find to Mason to see if he could cross-check that against US military men who have extreme climbing abilities along with that ink."

Erick nodded. "Noted. Before I forget, everyone must get back to me within forty-eight hours, even if just to tell me nothing further was found." Erick sighed, reading his meeting notes. "What about Tesla's further deconstruct on our tape recording of the new directive for our team's military truck, issued by the fake Corporal Shipley? And the bug set in our Afghanistan supplier's workshop?"

Badger answered. "I haven't heard from Tesla on either point. Kat, did she call you when I was under the knife?"

Kat shook her head. "Not me."

"Since Kat won't let me hold a phone"—Badger smiled wickedly in her direction—"I suggest Geir call Tesla for a follow-up on both those matters."

"Will do," Geir said with a nod.

"Okay, moving on," Erick said, "Our retired navy informant, Ben Chambers, was shot down in front of Badger, by the paid sniper. Then Badger killed our sniper when he visited Badger's hotel room. The sniper's photo was given to Mason and Levi for a full workup. I've spoken to both of them, but they have had no luck yet. I suspect we may need to contact Jonas at MI6 because our sniper may have been an international bad guy."

Erick continued, "And while we are talking about our folks across the pond—and since we have no contact info on the rebel leader who Cade, Laszlo and I met while in Afghanistan—does anybody know if Mason or Levi or even Bullard have somebody in the Kabul area to follow up with our friendly arms dealer? That bug is still live, but we need eyes on the arms trader's customers to seek out who is our laughing land mine buyer. If nobody's available to hang around, do we dare involve Shadowbox in this?"

Badger spoke up. "Let me handle that."

Kat said, "No, you won't be handling anything. Have that Merk guy or Brandon do it the next time they call you."

The room gave a collective laugh at how easily Kat would rein in Badger.

Talon shook his head and smiled. "I'll handle it, Kat."

Erick cleared his throat to cover up his chuckle. "Unless I've missed something, that takes care of the old stuff. Now here's the newest update. We've done an initial but full workup on Mouse," Erick said, returning to the business at hand. "We've got a list of everybody he ever came in contact with that we could find. And, I have to admit, it's not much. So I suggest what we do right now is, everybody tell me *everything* they might have heard or knew about Mouse. I thought I knew him pretty well. But honestly, when I tried to dredge up some memories, it was a lot of ribbing and teasing and bugging. I thought his family was from Texas. As far as I knew, he only had a mother."

Cade leaned forward, a frown on his face. "That can't be right. I swear to God he was from California and that he lived with his parents before hitting the military."

Badger looked at the two of them. "Really?"

Erick glanced over at him. "What do you remember?"

Badger frowned. "I was closer to him than all of you. I thought he had only an uncle in Texas. But I don't remember him being very willing to talk about him."

"Do you remember why?" Laszlo asked.

"No, but he was pretty adamant. I just can't remember if he gave me a specific reason or not. The thing about Mouse was, he always made up stories. It was pretty hard to tell what was real and what wasn't," Badger admitted. "But he was young. He was trying hard to be one of us. He would eventually turn into a hell of a man and be a great member of the unit, but we all know he wasn't quite there yet."

The men all nodded.

"That's quite true," Erick said. "We covered for him many times, and we helped him to make the grade as many times as we could. But he always knew he wasn't as good as the rest of us."

"But we never bugged him about that," Cade said.

And again the men nodded in agreement.

Erick wondered about that. "Do you think he wrote to his uncle, or to whoever was in his world who's trying to get back at us, that we were less than supportive?"

That topic brought up silence all around.

"He might have," Talon offered. "Any teasing we did was in the same vein as the teasing we always did. It was lighthearted, and we never meant any of the insults. It was the way of the world—our world particularly," Talon said. "Mouse always was pale. Remember that?" he added with a crooked grin. "We used to tease him about needing to spend time in the sun to gain a bit of color."

"I remember that, and he hated coffee. He's the only one of us who didn't drink coffee." Erick smiled with the memories. The others all pitched in with the bits and pieces they knew about Mouse as Erick wrote it all down. He realized it was all disjointed, and nobody had a clear sense of Mouse's beginnings. "Do you think he did that on purpose?"

"Did what?" Cade asked.

"Deliberately shrouded his history?" Erick stated. "Or maybe created different histories in order to make him feel better about his life?"

"He didn't have an easy childhood, I know that," Badger said suddenly. "His body was quite scarred."

The men frowned, thinking about that.

"Did he go into the navy to escape, do you think?" Kat asked.

Badger shrugged. "I wouldn't be at all surprised."

"And then the question becomes, to get away from what?" Kat asked.

Badger said quietly, "Every time I rack my brain to think of someone Mouse might have mentioned on his leaves, my mind draws a blank."

"What about girlfriends?" Clary asked. Her question landed in the middle of the group like a stone in a pond. Almost as if ripples of shock moved outward continuously.

Laszlo studied her for a long moment. "Mouse was gay."

She raised her eyebrows. "That could not have been easy in the military."

He shook his head. "Not only was it not easy, he took a

lot of razzing because of it. Not from us," he assured her hurriedly. "Not on that issue. But from a lot of the other guys."

"So maybe you guys weren't all targeted," she said quietly.

"Maybe Mouse was," Kat interjected. "How bad was it for somebody like Mouse?"

The men exchanged glances.

"Before he joined our unit, it was bad," Badger said.

"Suicidally bad?" asked Honey, her voice soft, gentle. "I'm sure the comments and actions would have hurt him inside, even if he didn't let anyone see his reaction."

Erick shrugged. "We never asked him about his sexuality that I know of." He glanced around the room. "At least I didn't. Did anyone here?"

All the men shook their heads.

"No, we never did," Badger said.

"So, if he didn't have any girlfriends, what do you know about his boyfriends?" Clary asked. "Because, if it wasn't a family member, we already know it's somebody who feels very strongly about Mouse. And that usually means it's a lover. Do you guys know who loved Mouse? Did he have anybody in his life? Did he have a permanent relationship or any off-and-on relationships?" She turned to stare at them. "Surely if you were all best friends and you know so much about each other, you'd know as much about Mouse?"

One by one they all turned to look at each other, then cast their gazes downward.

"He didn't talk to us," Badger said quietly. "I don't think he was ashamed as much as he was afraid of being humiliated or embarrassed, like he always had been."

"How long was he with you before the accident?"

Laszlo sighed. "One year. And in that year we couldn't convince him that he was safe with us."

"But obviously he wasn't safe," Talon said quietly. "Not when he's the only one dead."

Laszlo asked, "So where do I go next?"

"You?" Talon asked. "Why you?"

"Because you're laid up. So I'm the one who'll lead this next mission," he snapped. "And I'm totally okay if Geir comes along. But where are we going?"

"You'll go to Texas," Erick said quietly. "If that's where Mouse is from."

"Done," Laszlo said. "I'll head to Texas and find out for sure."

"And then what?" Clary asked.

"And then we'll start really tearing apart poor Mouse's life," Laszlo said. "Way deeper than we have done so far."

Clary nodded. "When you find whoever loves him, go easy. It's hard to lose someone you care about."

Laszlo's smile was diamond hard. "So very true. But it's also no excuse to go around killing others who loved him too."

This concludes Book 4 of SEALs of Steel: Talon.

Read about Laszlo: SEALs of Steel, Book 5

SEALS OF STEEL: LASZLO BOOK 5

When an eight-man unit hit a landmine, all were injured but one died. The remaining seven aim to see Mouse's death avenged.

As a child, Minx's best friend was Mouse. She hasn't heard from him in years, but she's never forgotten him.

Laszlo wonders if the whole squad was targeted, or just their youngest, newest member? Minx may be the only person who knew the boy that later became a dangerous, hunted man…

Book 5 is available now!

To find out more visit Dale Mayer's website.

http://smarturl.it/dmlaszlo

Author's Note

Thank you for reading Talon: SEALs of Steel, Book 4! If you enjoyed the book, please take a moment and leave a short review.

Dear reader,

I love to hear from readers, and you can contact me at my website: www.dalemayer.com or at my Facebook author page. To be informed of new releases and special offers, sign up for my newsletter or follow me on BookBub. And if you are interested in joining Dale Mayer's Fan Club, here is the Facebook sign up page.
facebook.com/groups/402384989872660

Cheers,
Dale Mayer

Your Free Book Awaits!

KILL OR BE KILLED

Part of an elite SEAL team, Mason takes on the dangerous jobs no one else wants to do – or can do. When he's on a mission, he's focused and dedicated. When he's not, he plays as hard as he fights.

Until he meets a woman he can't have but can't forget. Software developer, Tesla lost her brother in combat and has no intention of getting close to someone else in the military. Determined to save other US soldiers from a similar fate, she's created a program that could save lives. But other countries know about the program, and they won't stop until they get it – and get her.

Time is running out… For her… For him… For them…

DOWNLOAD a ***complimentary*** copy of MASON? Just tell me where to send it!

http://dalemayer.com/sealsmason/

About the Author

Dale Mayer is a USA Today bestselling author best known for her Psychic Visions and Family Blood Ties series. Her contemporary romances are raw and full of passion and emotion (Second Chances, SKIN), her thrillers will keep you guessing (By Death series), and her romantic comedies will keep you giggling (It's a Dog's Life and Charmin Marvin Romantic Comedy series).

She honors the stories that come to her – and some of them are crazy and break all the rules and cross multiple genres!

To go with her fiction, she also writes nonfiction in many different fields with books available on resume writing, companion gardening and the US mortgage system. She has recently published her Career Essentials Series. All her books are available in print and ebook format.

Connect with Dale Mayer Online

Dale's Website – www.dalemayer.com

Twitter – @DaleMayer

Facebook – facebook.com/DaleMayer.author

BookBub – bookbub.com/authors/dale-mayer

Also by Dale Mayer

Published Adult Books:

Psychic Vision Series

Tuesday's Child
Hide 'n Go Seek
Maddy's Floor
Garden of Sorrow
Knock Knock…
Rare Find
Eyes to the Soul
Now You See Her
Shattered
Into the Abyss
Seeds of Malice
Eye of the Falcon
Itsy-Bitsy Spider
Psychic Visions Books 1–3
Psychic Visions Books 4–6
Psychic Visions Books 7–9

By Death Series

Touched by Death
Haunted by Death
Chilled by Death
By Death Books 1–3

Charmin Marvin Romantic Comedy Series

Broken Protocols
Broken Protocols 2
Broken Protocols 3
Broken Protocols 3.5
Broken Protocols 1-3

Broken and... Mending

Skin
Scars
Scales (of Justice)
Broken but… Mending 1-3

Glory

Genesis
Tori
Celeste
Glory Trilogy

Biker Blues

Biker Blues: Morgan, Part 1
Biker Blues: Morgan, Part 2
Biker Blues: Morgan, Part 3
Biker Baby Blues: Morgan, Part 4
Biker Blues: Morgan, Full Set
Biker Blues: Salvation, Part 1
Biker Blues: Salvation, Part 2
Biker Blues: Salvation, Part 3
Biker Blues: Salvation, Full Set

SEALs of Honor

Mason: SEALs of Honor, Book 1

Hawk: SEALs of Honor, Book 2
Dane: SEALs of Honor, Book 3
Swede: SEALs of Honor, Book 4
Shadow: SEALs of Honor, Book 5
Cooper: SEALs of Honor, Book 6
Markus: SEALs of Honor, Book 7
Evan: SEALs of Honor, Book 8
Mason's Wish: SEALs of Honor, Book 9
Chase: SEALs of Honor, Book 10
Brett: SEALs of Honor, Book 11
Devlin: SEALs of Honor, Book 12
Easton: SEALs of Honor, Book 13
Ryder: SEALs of Honor, Book 14
Macklin: SEALs of Honor, Book 15
Corey: SEALs of Honor, Book 16
Warrick: SEALs of Honor, Book 17
SEALs of Honor, Books 1–3
SEALs of Honor, Books 4–6
SEALs of Honor, Books 7–10
SEALs of Honor, Books 11–13

Heroes for Hire

Levi's Legend: Heroes for Hire, Book 1
Stone's Surrender: Heroes for Hire, Book 2
Merk's Mistake: Heroes for Hire, Book 3
Rhodes's Reward: Heroes for Hire, Book 4
Flynn's Firecracker: Heroes for Hire, Book 5
Logan's Light: Heroes for Hire, Book 6
Harrison's Heart: Heroes for Hire, Book 7
Saul's Sweetheart: Heroes for Hire, Book 8
Dakota's Delight: Heroes for Hire, Book 9
Tyson's Treasure: Heroes for Hire, Book 10

Jace's Jewel: Heroes for Hire, Book 11
Rory's Rose: Heroes for Hire, Book 12
Brandon's Bliss: Heroes for Hire, Book 13
Liam's Lily: Heroes for Hire, Book 14
Heroes for Hire, Books 1–3
Heroes for Hire, Books 4–6
Heroes for Hire, Books 7–9

SEALs of Steel

Badger: SEALs of Steel, Book 1
Erick: SEALs of Steel, Book 2
Cade: SEALs of Steel, Book 3
Talon: SEALs of Steel, Book 4
Laszlo: SEALs of Steel, Book 5
Geir: SEALs of Steel, Book 6
Jager: SEALs of Steel, Book 7
The Last Wish: SEALs of Steel, Book 8

Collections

Dare to Be You…
Dare to Love…
Dare to be Strong…
RomanceX3

Standalone Novellas

It's a Dog's Life
Riana's Revenge
Second Chances

Published Young Adult Books:

Family Blood Ties Series

Vampire in Denial
Vampire in Distress
Vampire in Design
Vampire in Deceit
Vampire in Defiance
Vampire in Conflict
Vampire in Chaos
Vampire in Crisis
Vampire in Control
Vampire in Charge
Family Blood Ties Set 1–3
Family Blood Ties Set 1–5
Family Blood Ties Set 4–6
Family Blood Ties Set 7–9
Sian's Solution, A Family Blood Ties Series Prequel Novelette

Design series

Dangerous Designs
Deadly Designs
Darkest Designs
Design Series Trilogy

Standalone

In Cassie's Corner
Gem Stone (a Gemma Stone Mystery)
Time Thieves

Published Non-Fiction Books:

Career Essentials

Career Essentials: The Résumé

Career Essentials: The Cover Letter

Career Essentials: The Interview

Career Essentials: 3 in 1

CPSIA information can be obtained
at www.ICGtesting.com
Printed in the USA
FFHW010732260419
52057574-57443FF